Tales of the Fall
Book I

Onlyness

J.A. Wynn

A MediaCrash Book

Published by MediaCrash Books

PUBLISHER'S NOTE
This is a work of fiction. Names, characters, places, and incidents either are the product of the author's imagination or are used fictitiously, and any resemblance to actual persons, living or dead, events, or locales is entirely coincidental.

Library of Congress Catalog Card Number: PENDING

ISBN: 978-0-9821837-1-7

Second (Revised) Edition: July 2016

1 2 3 4 5 6 7 8 9 10 IN 20 19 18 17 16

***

Dedicated to the children of the world, of all ages.
They are our last great hope for rescue.

***

Contents

CONTENTS

The First Tale

The Fall of Corrina

Chapter 1

The Traveler

*Of the beginnings of the prophecy
and of the curse that was given*

A SINGLE traveler walked lamely on a deserted path. He was clad in a filthy, tattered cloak, which he pulled tightly to himself to ward off the mountain winds. His body was broken with age and his face showed the etchings of years spent in toil and hardship. Only his eyes were youthful. Animated and bright, they scanned the trail ahead for a sign of shelter. Darkness was quickly approaching and the traveler knew that his chances of surviving the night in such a desolate place were slim. At last, he spied a light! Faint and flickering, a distant glow emanated from what must have been a window or door, and where there were windows and doors, the traveler reasoned, there were usually walls. Summoning the dregs of the day's strength, he trudged on.

Presently, he saw that the light originated from a small and solitary inn that sat just to one side of the path. With firm resolve, for he already felt the warmth of the fire inside, he breached the door and began to remove his cloak.

"Hullo, fellows," he said cautiously. "Might a weary old man get a pint and a morsel from ye kind folks? I've traveled many a path today and yours are the first faces I've seen."

"Aye, kind we are but frugal as well, old man," replied the innkeeper. "Show me the coin you'll pay with and I'll see that you're fed." The innkeeper saw the threadbare condition of the traveler's cloak and prepared to unceremoniously eject him. "I am not in the business of charity," he said. He put his hand on the old man's shoulder as if to force him back into the cold.

"Hold, sir, I beg you. I admit I have no coin, but I have something far more valuable to barter." The wizened old man saw that his only chance lay in the sympathy, or perhaps the curiosity, of the innkeeper and his patrons. He hoped that the luck that had brought him to the inn before night's descent was still with him. The innkeeper took a step back and glanced at his customers. They waited expectantly. Myth and superstition were strong in them and the old man had the look of a wizard. They knew much better than to disbelieve.

"What do you have to trade then, if not silver or gold?" asked the innkeeper. He too had heard the stories about strange old men and was wary of bringing bad luck upon his house. "I see that you carry nothing with you, and that your days of trading labor are far behind you."

"What I offer is light enough for my stooped shoulders to carry easily," began the traveler, "yet so heavy that it can bend and break even the strongest back. I've carried it with me for many years now but I never fear to barter with it, for with each exchange both parties grow richer." He paused. The assembly in the room was leaning forward anxiously. He *was* a wizard! Only wizards and lunatics spoke this way and the man was so slightly built that, if he was a lunatic, he posed no threat.

"Well, what is it?" asked the innkeeper finally. His curiosity was aroused as well.

"I offer you knowledge," replied the old man. The room sagged. This was no wizard, this was a teacher. Teachers often spoke in riddles, but they usually had nothing of any real value. The customers turned back to their ale; there would be no magic amulet, nor would there be dancing girls produced. The occupants of the inn were woodcutters and soldiers, thieves and vagabonds. They had the knowledge that they needed to perform their trades and they chose not to be distracted from their relaxation by more of the same. The innkeeper rolled his eyes and stepped forward. "Hold!" commanded the old man in a surprisingly strong voice. "I offer you a tale."

The innkeeper stepped back and once again awaited the judgment of his customers. He could already sense their eagerness. Tales were rare and valuable commodities, used to entertain and to educate, to pacify and to terrify. A good tale was easily worth a meal and a night's lodging. One of the patrons scrambled to furnish the tired wanderer with a chair, while another took his cloak. A mug of ale was thrust into his hand as the door was shut behind him. The men, who had finished their meals, lit pipes and settled back into their seats as the fire was stoked and banked. The innkeeper's wife called her children from the kitchen in case the story had a moral and the young scullery maid cocked an ear as she worked, in the hopes that the story had a dashing hero.

"We haven't heard a good tale in many a month, stranger," laughed the innkeeper. "I hope that it's got dragons in it."

"Not dragons...demons," spoke the storyteller in a low voice. "And the Devil himself."

A shiver swept through the inn as the gathering considered this. A few muttered hurried prayers to their favorite saints and the innkeeper's wife covered her children's ears and shooed them back into the kitchen.

"Oh," replied the innkeeper, "it is a serious tale then?"

"Aye, serious...and deep," said the storyteller, "and all the more so because it is true."

"True?" asked the innkeeper. "Pray tell, how do you know that this story of demons and devils is true." He looked at the storyteller in cautious disbelief.

"Because it is my own story." There was a soft, quick intake of breath from the gathering; the storyteller felt the collected eyes focus more intensely on him. "Sit back and learn as I relate it..."

"There is a place that is pain for the Damned. A place where the torment paid in retribution for a lifetime of sin is real and everlasting. It is a place of revelry and celebration for the fallen divinities, it is their haven and a dark prince is their lord. His power is unchallenged between his borders and he rules over his vassals from within a coal-black pit in the deepest recesses of Hell. His form is sometimes that of a cat or a stag, or of a goat-horned giant, but he will also wear mortal flesh if he chooses.

"His court is held in a chamber, which is ornamented with tin, copper and bronze, but he lacks not wealth. In this chamber is his throne and before this throne is a pool of liquid fire that, if gazed into, reflects all that is above. The prince alone can use this magic, and with it he sees images of his own domain, glimpses of our human world, and sights of Heaven, too. He sees things past and things yet to come, and things of this very instant.

"Around this pool dance the Succubae, women beautiful and yet terrifying to behold. They are forever lost, harlots who have submitted fully to the darkness. They have followed the lure of flesh to the position that they now hold, condemned to dance shamelessly for the prince and his cohorts. They weave seductive paths between and around each other, close to the edge of the fiery pool, glistening in the sweat of their exertions. Their eyes are first teasing and coquettish, a moment later tortured and glaring madly as they gyrate and swoon for the pleasure of demons.

"Behind the prince's right shoulder stand two creatures. One of these is Andras. He appears as a grim soldier, with a fierce visage, wearing a red helm and cloak. He is an ancient and powerful sorcerer and his is the power to twist and weave spells.

"Next to Andras stands an angel of black. He is Berith, the archduke of Hell. Sly and clever, he is a friend to Andras and he, too, is strong in the techniques of High Magic. He is known to be the more cunning of the two and is adept in the arts of intrigue. Together they are the Devil's Ministers, and are second only to the prince in their unholy power.

"This is a tale of the blackest court and of the deceptions of its courtiers. It is a story of lustful infatuations, potent rages and envy. The truth is buried inside of it."

THE STORYTELLER paused and leaned back on his stool. A hush had fallen over the inn and the creak and groan of the stool as it tilted cracked the silence. The gathered people blinked and released a unified breath as the storyteller loosened his hold on their attention. The innkeeper motioned to his wife. She hurried to the storyteller's table and replenished his mug of ale, her eyes wide and still fastened to him. He took a long pull at his mug and swabbed his ragged sleeve across his lips. From beneath heavy brows, his piercing eyes softened and seemed to drift into reverie. He went on.

"In an age that is long past us now, in the worlds inhabited by demons and angels, there once was a passion great enough to curse a demon's soul. It began as an unholy lust, yet it flowered into a love pure enough to cause a demon to seek repentance. The seed of it was planted in such an evil place, of *that* you can be sure. It is Hell that I speak of, for it is there that this tale truly begins.

"Imagine a being that appears as a giant, sinewy, copper-skinned man. Twisted goat's horns protrude from his brow. He sits, brooding in his chamber, atop his black throne, and gazes unflinching into the flaming pool before him. His attention never wavers from this pool, even when one of his many women offers herself to him. He seems possessed by the vision in the flames. None but he can see the scene that has him ensnared so tightly, but the occupants of the chamber can sense the tension inside of him. Finally, a voice, first hesitantly and then resolutely, resounds through the court-room.

"' My Lord, what is it that you see in the flame? Never before have I seen you so enthralled by the vision that you find in it.' It was the voice of Berith that finally shook the glamour from the prince's eyes. He slowly closed his eyes once, then again, as if to cleanse them of an irritation. The muscles of his back clenched as he stretched himself, cat-like. At last he turned and addressed his duke.

"' I see a woman, Berith. In truth, she is no more than a girl. A mortal girl.'

"Berith, realizing then that his Lord was free of his self-induced spell, stepped from behind the throne and strode to the center of the chamber. He stopped and stood still, considering what he was about to say.

"After a moment, he spoke. 'Lord, forgive my imperti-nence. I realize that it is not my place to question you, but I am curious. It is unusual that you hold such interest in a mortal. You've not taken your eyes from her since what must have been her birth. Who is this girl?'

"The prince fixed his eyes on Berith, a faithful servant to him since his reign began. Berith stared fearlessly back, wondering if he had upset his master and prepared for an explosion of rage.

"But the prince nodded and sighed. 'I do not mistake your curiosity for impertinence, Berith. The affairs of this principality are of a concern to you and for that I am thank-ful. I must admit that I've neglected my office somewhat in order to spy like a schoolboy on this mortal. It must and will end today, for today I've decided.' He stood and beckoned to Berith. 'Come closer, duke. And you too, Andras. Come and peer over my shoulder at this glorious morsel. In all eternity, I've seen none like this.'

"Berith and Andras glanced quickly at one another; thinly veiled anticipation surged through them both. Their master was obviously excited. He seldom spoke this much, and an invitation to see through the magic of the pool was unheard of. There were none who held more favor in the eyes of the prince than Berith and Andras, but in an eternity of service neither had seen more than tongues of flame in the pool. They both stepped forward eagerly.

"'Look at her!' bellowed the prince, clapping his palms together. The flames shot up and out of the pool to shower onto his giant frame. He reared back his head and laughed into the spout of flame as the flesh of his shoulders started to crack and singe. His advisors moved back, not out of fear of the flames but out of a fear of their master. Most of his magics were still unknown to them and they had learned long ago to be cautious. The prince started to swallow the flame as it poured over him; it began to consume him from within. Small holes opened in his skin, letting tendrils of fire lick out. He sucked in mightily and the holes widened, pouring light from his wounds. The light from the flame quickly lost its reddish hue and became blue, then white-hot. Of the prince there was nothing left but his laughter, which echoed throughout the chamber, resonating through the white glow. Then, even his laughter died, leaving just whiteness above the now empty pool.

"Andras and Berith stood entranced as the whiteness started to coalesce into a human form. Slowly, the form hardened into the shape of a dancing woman, on the cusp of her eighteenth year perhaps. Her face was turned away from the demons as she materialized, but she swung grace-fully and purposefully towards them as the steps of her dance dictated. As she faced the pair, they gasped. Her beauty was astonishing, their eyes were riveted to her per-fect figure as she performed. The most complex movements she executed flawlessly, and she wore an expression of such unspoiled serenity that her movements seemed to require no more difficulty than the drawing of a breath.

"In a daze, Andras moved forward and extended his hand to touch her. Lecherous thoughts rose in his demon's mind. A beauty so unblemished and so near to him was more than he could withstand. His trembling fingertips brushed her lips as she spun close…

"And, suddenly, the prince reappeared, his man's head atop a serpent's body, poised over Andras' outstretched hand. Venom ran in rivulets down his chin as he reared back to strike. The red-robed wizard made an attempt to pull away but the prince's fangs slid into his skin. He screamed and cursed, then fell to his knees.

"'Spare me from this torment, Sire. I knew not what I did!' cried Andras, clutching his bleeding hand to his breast. 'Let me die, Sire, I beg you!' he howled, his eyes spinning madly in his head.

"'You will not die, Andras,' pronounced the prince calmly. 'You will feel the fire of the venom inside you as you contemplate your misdeed. For now, at least, you will leave us.' And with a gesture from the prince, the wizard was gone from the courtroom. The prince had shed his serpent's skin and was once again a huge, horned man.

"Berith had witnessed the banishment unflinchingly. He, too, had been tempted by the vision of the girl, but he had restrained himself. He knew only too well the punishments that the dark prince could inflict and reserved his sympathy for his own transgressions. He waited as his master resumed his accustomed place on the throne.

"'Did you see her beauty, Berith? Am I wrong in proclaiming her?' asked the prince. 'Their lives are so fleeting, no more than a grain of sand in an hourglass. I must have her, and soon.'

"The black wizard had known that he would want the girl. He would foul her and when she was spoiled, she would join his harem, destined to an eternal dance in Hell's pit. Berith began to formulate a scheme."

THE FIRE EBBED LOW in the inn and the gathered company crowded closer to the storyteller as if the shrinking ring of warmth and light was a noose that tightened around them. The innkeeper saw that the storyteller had knife and fork in hand and was distracted.

He ventured a question. "The devil would try to take her?" he whispered.

The storyteller swallowed a mouthful and spoke, "During the time of these happenings, traffic between the worlds of men and demons was common. Be warned! It could be common once again! It is through no action of ours that the devil-hordes are kept at bay, it is only their own indifference to our affairs. This indifference and their own petty squabbling are our sole protection, and cursed is the one who garners their attention. To be the subject of a Devil-King's infatuation is a curse indeed, and a fate not to be contemplated lightly. But contemplate it you must if you wish to tread the path that this tale uncovers."

Chapter 2

The Seduction

*Of the wooing of Corrina
and of the failed seduction*

BERITH WASTED NO TIME in beginning his treachery. He summoned a lesser demon and retired to his chamber. The seduction of the mortal woman would require a subtlety honed through eons of wickedness, a masterful plot of evil. He knew already the shape that the girl's downfall would take and he sat silently in meditation and waited for the fallen angel to arrive. He opened his eyes as a form manifested before him.

"Greetings, my Lord, you summoned me?" announced the being that shimmered into solidity.

"Ahhh...Sitri, I have a task for you. Something that you, of all the angels in Hell, are perfectly suited for." He appraised the demon, and rose from his seated position to glide menacingly across the room. "Have you been to the mortal realm in my service?" he asked. He bent to peer into a small, murky crystal ball that was held by a living creature atop a stand in the center of the room.

"No, my Lord, not on a mission for you, but I have been many times." The demon was human in appearance, yet unearthly in demeanor. He was attired in the manner of a gentleman soldier, well coiffed and polished. Despite the elegance of his bearing, he exuded an air of malevolent danger that seemed to project from his darkened eyes. Berith turned to face him.

"Then this will be a great opportunity for both of us to prove our worth to our Master, will it not? I have watched for ages as you have had your way with the fragile, delicate, mortal beasts and I have always found your particular style of cruelty inspiring. Would you be willing to enter into my service in the unholy name of our prince and Master?" He fixed his gaze firmly on his subordinate, his expression making it clear that his request was not an option. Sitri returned the glare with one of his own, his eyes filled with arrogance and pride.

"Thy will be done, my Lord," he said, "in the name of our Master. What would you have me do?"

Berith returned to his seat in front of Sitri, forming his fingers into a pyramid, the tips touching his chin. He carefully measured his words, a hint of warning on his lips. "It is a woman, Sitri. In truth, a mortal girl. You are to seduce her and turn her heart to impurity. Is this something you would do in the service of our prince?" His tone was ominous, forbidding. "You understand what is required?" The question was filled with danger.

Sitri responded cautiously. "I am to incarnate on the Earthly plane and turn a mortal toward temptation, influence her to lust?" He sensed something more in Berith's request, a deeper meaning perhaps. "Is that all, Lord?"

"No, Sitri. *You* will seduce her. *You* will become the object of her lust. *You* will consummate her sin." Berith paused to see the effect of his words on the lesser being and folded his gnarled hands.

"My Lord…" began Sitri slowly, "that is forbidden by The Most High. That is why we are here now…"

Berith cut him off angrily, "When shall it be proper for an angel to question an Archangel?" he snapped. "Are the thrones and principalities still in their accustomed places? What is thy answer?" He waited, seething.

"We are fallen, Lord," said Sitri. "Not thrones or principalities…Fallen." He mustered his dignity and composed himself, "However, I am sorry for my insolence. It is much too late for us all. Who is this mortal and where shall I find her? My answer is yes. I will tempt this mortal beast." With shame in his eyes, he lowered his face to the floor.

Dismissively, Berith waved him toward the crystal, the outburst momentarily forgotten. Sitri looked into the shadowy depths of the ball and saw the girl. His eyes widened. The effect of her exquisite grace and beauty was immediate. Entranced by the vision inside the glass, he nearly didn't respond to the last order given by the duke.

"Her name is Corrina de Rouen, Sitri. You leave at once, prepare thyself." Sitri reluctantly tore his eyes away from the crystal and straightened.

"Yes, my Lord. At once. Thy will be done," he said and vanished.

HE APPEARED AT THE EDGE of a darkened glade, swallowed by the shadows that bordered it. He crouched, hidden, and took in his surroundings. The small clearing in the forest was carpeted with twilight mist and slumbering ferns and the brooding trees were cloaked in moss.

He spied a figure in the circle, seated in the moonlight. Slender and silent, a girl was surrounded by a soft bluish light; the very air around where she sat was illuminated. A ring of toadstools was traced on the forest floor and, seated upon them with their heads bowed in deference to her, were a group of diminutive winged creatures. Sitri recognized them. In a way they were cousins to him and he regarded them warily. They were immune to the many powers he had brought into the world with him and they would not take kindly to his presence in their forest. They appeared to be waiting upon the girl, as if they were a court of sorts and she, a queen or princess. She seemed to assume the role naturally, with a sublime and easy grace.

Sitri's eyes were riveted on the scene before him, he watched as the girl rose to her delicate feet and bowed to the creatures. With a flutter of wings, they took to the air and formed a glowing halo around her face. A haunting, ethereal melody flowed from the cloud as the beings began to sing to her, spinning into an intricately patterned dance about her head. As the flying creatures established their rhythm, the girl began a dance of her own. Slowly, gently, the girl held her hands away from her sides and the little creatures held her fingers and pulled her with them. Sitri watched, enthralled by the dreamlike movements of the fairies as they led the girl deeper into the forest. To his demon's mind this was impossible. He knew that a mortal could never be pure enough to feel the hand of Faerie, yet already the girl was being lifted above the forest floor by tiny wings. He waited until the glowing cloud was beyond the furthest edge of the clearing before he cautiously followed.

The tangled branches parted before his advance as he followed the diffused, electrical light through the wood. Staying just out of the girl's vision, he kept pace with the floating dancer as she arched and twisted with the music of the fairies. His eyesight was attuned to the vague glow that was draped about her, he was a natural hunter and the midnight darkness of the forest was a comfort to him. He knew that he could never approach her while the fairies were singing for they would know him for what he was and react with hostile vengeance. The old feuds between their races would never be forgotten. No, he would wait until she was alone and the dance was done. The flickering creatures would not tarry in the mortal world for long; their time was long past. He knew that they would finish the song soon and then the girl would sleep.

She opened her eyes to the soft gleam of dawn as the pale, verdant light filtered into the glade. The fairies had led the dance in a long, luxurious circle throughout the wood, ending in the same cleared glade in which they had begun. They had laid her out on a cushion of moss, departing along with the last wisps of fog caught in the morning sun. She had dreamt of the song, as she always did when she danced with them in the forest and the song would haunt her throughout the following days. It was always there, yet just out of her reach, just beyond her making it more than a dream. It was never a part of her waking life and she lay back on the velvet moss to dream the song again.

She sat up suddenly, her eyes wide, her pulse quickened. This time, the tune was not a dream. She looked about her, toward the edges of the glade. There, she heard it again, a snatch of the Faerie song, drifting faintly through the trees. She pulled her arms around her, covering herself in alarm, her modesty coming to consciousness before she fully did. She held her hand to her mouth, stifling a tiny gasp, as she came to the awareness that she was not alone in the forest.

Sitri had never before seen a being as lovely as this mortal Corrina. He made a low whistle of the melody that he had heard, adding a darker, more sensual air to it. He remembered a time when he had been charged with the duty to sing in reverence and worship and the memory pained him. His rendering of the song became more sinister as it took on a minor key. He watched through the veil of leaves as Corrina rose to her feet and anxiously began to seek a path on which to flee. He stood as she did and she started in fright as he emerged from where he had been concealed.

"Don't be frightened…Don't run away," he said. His voice carried softly through the morning air, a touch of gentle reassurance floating along with it. Corrina stood timidly, trembling in the sudden presence of a stranger, ashamed that he had been watching as she slept. Her face flushed crimson as she struggled to regain her composure.

"Sir, would you please excuse me, I became lost in the wood last night," she said. "Now that it is light enough to see, I shall be able to find my way. If I were to be found in your company at this hour, it would be most embarrassing for me. I see that you are a gentleman, so I am certain that you will overlook my rudeness." She started to turn away from him while attempting to smooth her dress. "My family must be searching for me," she finished hurriedly. Averting her eyes, she brushed past him and ducked under the branches that edged the glade. He stepped aside as if to allow her to pass, then suddenly reached for her and held her firmly by a shoulder. She tugged at his grip but was unable to break away and she paused, shocked by his touch.

He murmured ancient syllables, summoning eldritch powers to his command and she felt a vibration pass through his hand and into her shoulders. Again, he whispered and she felt stillness, as though she were standing at the center of a whirlwind, a spinning vortex all around her. She looked up into his darkened eyes and saw nothing else; his eyes became her entire world. Her story began and ended within the confines of his eyes and she could neither imagine nor remember anything beyond them. His mesmerizing stare penetrated deep into her and held her frozen in the glade, her flight forgotten.

From somewhere inside the shadows of his gaze, she heard him speak. "I certainly shall overlook your rudeness, if you would only grant me one small favor. A trifle really, I'm sure you wouldn't refuse such a simple request." She hung limply in his arms, caught like a tiny butterfly in the spider-web of his stare. He went on, his tone compelling, "Just a dance...Dance with me as you danced last night."

He picked up a strong, exotic rhythm, tempestuous as only a demon could create. Pulling Corrina's rag-doll frame closer to him, he began a ghastly parody of the elegant, gentle dance of the Faerie. The spell that he wove was from before the dawn of man, from before the first seedlings had taken root in those woods. He stalked in slow, powerful lines, holding her tightly while tracing arcane symbols across the forest floor. A shadow fell across the glade as a dark cloud blocked the morning sun and the newly wakened songbirds fell silent. Corrina did not resist. Barely aware of her surroundings, she slipped into the pulse of the rhythm and followed the demon's lead. As the woods once again became dark, a brooding music resonated from the darkness. The musicians themselves remained hidden in the shadows, preferring to be unseen in the daylight hours. The staccato melody grew and intensified as she was swept along the pattern that the demon traced. Her heart was pounding furiously, yet she was calm and accommodating, leaning into Sitri as he performed his steps. What had happened to her? Who was this stranger? She was confused and terrified because her feet were following the stranger's unfamiliar dance. It was as though the dance had been rehearsed a thousand times before or had been choreographed by the two of them together. Even with the Faerie, it had never been like this. The song went on until Corrina grew tired and then, as her eyes became heavy, Sitri laid her back upon her bed of moss and she slumbered in the shadowy, silent glade.

As she slept, she dreamt of the new song, the song that she and the stranger had danced to. The dream was of a place filled with light, a glade hidden in the forest like the one she now lay in. In the dream, a chapel sat in the center of the glade and a rippling brook ran past where she lay. The chapel was built of white stone with a small wooden door beneath a tall white steeple. In her dream, she sat next to the brook, her hand dipped lazily in it, casting trails of bubbles through the soft current. She lifted her hand to drink, but before she did, she saw a shadow fall across the water. She looked up into the face of the stranger and saw that his hand was held out to her, waiting to help her to her feet. He was there to help her across the water. She looked down at the water in her hand and listened to the sound of the song, she struggled to make out the words. She began to look back into the eyes of the stranger, but as she did, the door of the chapel swung open. The song of Faerie swelled from within the chapel, drowning out the stranger's song, and she could hear individual voices singing inside, voices she knew, that belonged to ones she had danced with. She looked at the water cupped in her hand and brought it to her lips.

Her eyes snapped open just as Sitri's lips brushed hers and she pulled violently away, twisting her face to one side and scrambling to her knees.

"What are you doing? Stay away!" she exclaimed. She clambered across the ground, distancing herself from him and pressing her back against a knotted tree. "How dare you, sir! Who are you?"

Sitri was astonished, she should have awakened from the dream and melted into his arms. He quickly recovered and concealed his surprise from the furious maiden. She glared at him, her pretty face tightened into an expression of anger, her jaw set in defiance. He realized that she was ravishing when she was so distraught. It was actually disorienting how beautiful she was. He came to his senses and remembered his duty.

"Corrina, my dearest... You and I belong together. Come, let me show you my love. I want to give you the world." His voice was silken smooth and sweet, entreating as he crept toward her. "I have loved you from afar for so long now. Let me kiss you." As he moved close to her and slid his hands around her slight form she suddenly struck him with a resounding slap. The sound of it rang throughout the forest, sending birds twittering into the air. He recoiled as if stung, a perplexed look spreading across his face.

"How do you know my name? Who are you?" she demanded angrily. "I will kill you if you come near me again," she stated flatly. She glowered at him, trying her best to appear intimidating but only succeeding in appearing even more beautiful. The demon was dumbfounded; the spell he had used was infallible. He was irresistible. His magic was perfected and he had never failed his master. He scanned the unfathomable depths of his memory for a solution and none appeared. He slowly sat back in defeat.

"My name is Sitri," he began slowly, unsure of himself. His mind raced, considering the punishments he might re-

ceive for failing. "I have watched you dance here before."
He could not force himself upon her, for that would not fulfill Berith's command. He could not harm her. He could not
return as a failure. He was at a loss. "I thought, when I saw
you, that you must be an angel, come to Earth. I wanted to
hold a thing so perfect."

"Thing? I am no thing!" she said hotly, "Only a fool
would approach a decent lady in that manner!" She rose
to her feet, less frightened now. "And it is blasphemy to
say that any beside the Lord is perfect." She pushed back
her golden hair and glanced at the strange man at her feet.
He kept his face toward the ground and remained still. Her
heart softened. "Sir, I am flattered, but I was not to be in
these woods. If you care as you say you do, then mention
this to no one. Please, I beg of you. Do not follow me, and do
not spy on us again. Forget what was a dream that you only
thought was real. Forget..." Sitri, the fallen angel, raised his
face only to catch the faintest glimmer of gold as she disappeared between the trees.

Chapter 3

The Anchor

Of The Anchor of Flesh
and of Sitri's betrayal

SITRI sat stunned in the forest. Completely astounded at the events that had just transpired, he could not fathom returning to his master's presence. To arrive without the girl would cause uproar in Hell and to fail in a mission of this importance would result in dire penalties. To be a demon was penalty enough and Sitri had no mind to step willingly into another banishment. He searched his memory for any loophole, any trick that would make the girl bend to his will, but his search was in vain. The girl was beyond the power of his magic, and that in itself was inexplicable. He stood and paced to and fro across the clearing, stroking the stubble of beard on his chin. The whiskers were grown to the exact length and shade that would normally drive a young maiden to passionate madness, but even they had failed him. How could this have happened? To him! The legendary Sitri, spurned and tossed aside. And by an unexceptional mortal no less. At that thought Sitri paused, the girl was certainly exceptional. He was forced to admit the fact. She was like no one he had ever seen; her face was already haunting his thoughts. He could not return without her, he would have to enlist help. With that final thought, he moved his hand in a complex and cryptic gesture and vanished from the wood.

He rematerialized on a shadowed path, a set of stairs leading up and away from him. He was back in Hell, but had managed to remain unseen to the prince. The stairs were faded and crumbling and careened in a chaotic spiral toward a door, cut into a black stone wall. The wall seemed to curve away from the stairway and fade into nothingness, but the door was solid and foreboding. Sitri looked behind him as though to catch a glimpse of Corrina, but failing that, he turned and slowly began climbing the cracking stairs. A howling wind blasted from what seemed like every direction and threatened to tear him from the stairs but he continued on. So much of that place was simple illusion, and Sitri was quite fluent in threats and illusion himself. At last he came to the door and, grasping the large iron knocker, proceeded to announce his arrival.

After some time, a voice sounded from behind the door. "Is that Sitri that rails at our door so?" the disembodied voice asked.

"Yes, it is Sitri. Let me inside, I have a puzzle for you to solve." He looked nervously about as he waited for a response. The prince had agents everywhere in his realm, and although he was not omniscient, he certainly appeared to be at times. Sitri knew that his time was short and that his presence in Hell would soon be reported.

The voices spoke again, "Enter cousin, you are always welcome in our chambers. Come and tell us of your puzzle." The door swung open and Sitri entered. Before him in the darkened room stood two figures, aged and decrepit. The Ministers, Berith and Andras, loomed over the instruments of torture and sorcery that were the tools of their craft. Their current forms were those of two wizened old men; they eyed Sitri with interest and beckoned him forward. "What is this puzzle that you speak of?" asked Andras.

"About the mission that I was dispatched to the Earthly plane to complete," he began. "The girl that I was to retrieve?"

"Yes, we remember…how goes the seduction?" asked Berith. "Some of us are not so lucky as others, Sitri. We enjoy the pleasures of flesh vicariously through you." Berith licked his cracked and flaking lips and smiled evilly. "All goes well, I hope."

"The girl refused me, Berith," snapped Sitri. "I have no idea why. It's unbelievable really and our lord will not be pleased. You must help me."

Both of the ancient sorcerers burst into wicked laughter, their eyes glowing cruelly and narrowing in mirth. "Help *you*, Sitri, the favorite of our lord? How could we possibly help one who is so perfect and pretty? What is it that you could possibly need from tired, old conjurers such as we?" The wizards circled around a smoldering censer that dominated the room and cast handfuls of powder into the embers around it. "Why should we?" finished Andras.

"I know that there is no affection between us," started Sitri, "yet I feel that nothing would be gained by allowing our lord to be denied his will. If he does not receive the soul of this maiden, he will surely punish the lot of us." He eyed the sorcerers cautiously, a small glimmer of hope arising in him. They seemed to consider his words. Both sorcerers stared into the smoke that swirled into the darkness that hid the ceiling high above them, they murmured and whispered to each other as they assessed the situation that Sitri described. After a time they looked away from the smoke and each other and back at Sitri.

Berith spoke first. "Yes, Sitri, you are correct. There is nothing for any of us to gain by your failure and raising the ire of our master benefits no one, yet how do you propose that we solve this 'puzzle'? How can we achieve the very thing that a master such as you cannot? We are not versed in the arts of love; our skills are quite different, as I'm sure you are aware. We are adept at more, shall we say, *forcible* techniques." He glanced at Andras, his eyes darting between the other wizard and the demon before him. "Do you propose that we force the girl?"

"No! She cannot be forced against her will for that would not affect the soul. She must be convinced that this is what she wants; she must be willing." Sitri paced the floor of the chamber, agitated. He ground his fist into his palm and looked up. "You must have knowledge of some solution!"

Andras spoke with a sideways warning, "We have knowledge to be sure, Sitri, do not underestimate us. We are simply clarifying what exactly it is that you desire. Speak candidly with us, how do you think we should go about this? Magic is not a thing of science, it is a thing of will. You must have a part in this or it will never be successful. What is it that you wish? Speak it and we shall be able to conjure it. We are merely the conduits to your desire." The wizards waited expectantly.

"I am no magician!" burst out Sitri. "I do not know the ways that such things are done! How am I to speak of what I do not know?" He was impatient and anxious and his frustration became obvious. "You answer a riddle with more of the same!"

"We know that you are no wizard, Sitri, we simply ask that you shape the spell with your mind. We will create it in ways that are beyond your understanding. Only, you must first create the vessel in your mind and form the cup that we shall pour the magic *into*. Think of what it is that you request, for you have seen such things before."

Sitri looked upward into the dark eyes of the Ministers and for a moment he saw a deep abyss, stretching into infinite blackness before him. There was cold in the staring eyes of the wizards that chilled even the icy heart of the demon. After an instant of hesitation, he cleared his throat and spoke. "I seek a love potion. I seek a charm that will make the girl desire me. Or to make me desirable to her. Do you know of such a spell?" He looked down at the floor of the chamber in shame, his pride wounded.

"There it is, Sitri. That wasn't so hard, was it? A simple request and we can to begin to solve *our* puzzle. And it is our puzzle, Sitri, because you are quite right. There would be nothing to gain in your failure. An angry overlord is not needed in a place such as this, and we must all look after one another, mustn't we?" Berith stepped away from the smoke that rose from the censer and moved toward Sitri as he reached into the folds of his robe. "I have just the thing for you. A charm to grant you what you desire." From within his robe, he produced a small stone with arcane symbols etched into one side and a thick silver chain wound through a hole near one edge. "Andras, do you think that this will do?" He tossed the stone to the other wizard who snatched it from the air with his gnarled hand.

"Ahhh…yes…yes, this will do nicely, I'm sure. I have not seen this particular piece for centuries, this will do nicely." Andras cradled it lovingly in his hand and looked at it appraisingly, "This is exactly what you need, Sitri, precisely what you require. A love charm." He nonchalantly tossed it through the smoky air to Sitri, who reached out and caught it by the chain. It hung, swinging in the bluish haze of the incense, reflecting the muted glow of the embers. Sitri held it up to his face to look at the symbols that were carved into it.

"How does it work?" he asked. The sorcerers slid around the chamber speaking together, over one another, their voices merging into a single droning sound.

"You must wear it from now until you return and you must not remove it while you are in the mortal realm." As the wizards spoke, beneath their mixed voices was another voice, deeper and speaking in other tongues. That voice was the same as the interwoven voices of the sorcerers, but louder and darker. Sitri realized that it was their true voice, ancient and malevolent. Not simply inhuman, but beyond demonic. The voice was something that he had never heard, even as a damned, fallen angel. The sorcerers continued, "You must put it around your neck even now, tonight, and you must make the maiden touch it. She must not read the sigils that are upon it or the spell will be broken. If you do these things, you will be irresistible to her." The other voice stopped. Sitri brought the stone to his face and slipped the chain over his head.

"Is there anything that I must do to make it work?" he asked.

The two wizards looked at each other and then at him and replied in unison, "You have already done your part."

Chapter 4

Submission

---

*Of Corrina's surrender
and of trust forsaken*

CORRINA could not sleep. She moved fitfully beneath the thin fabric of the coverlet that threatened to entangle her. The sweltering summer heat caused her to rise from her bed and to look outward into the evening. Above her, outside her window, the yellowed moon sat heavy in the sky and she glimpsed the glow of fireflies in the forest that bounded her family's land. To her left, in a cleft between the trees, was the head of the trail that led to the clearing in the woods where the arrogant stranger had accosted her the previous morning. She thought about it angrily; what shamelessness could cause a man to behave that way? Her father had been right all along; men *were* monsters and little more than animals, with the exception of him of course. She turned and walked back toward her bed, a feeling of dreaminess coming over her. The night was quiet and a sensation of timelessness permeated the air. Corrina, almost against her will, passed by her bed and, after closing her door softly behind her, walked by her father's closed door and stepped into the warm summer night.

Skirting the edge of the wood, she walked slowly around the limits of her father's holdings. Her father was well known in the surrounding region and was a man of respect and reputation. He was admired chiefly for the way that he had reared his children, to behave with admirable decorum and restraint. Corrina was the apple of his eye, a sculpture of beauty and elegance, yet still pious and respectful. She was destined for the convent or the mission for she was both reverent and chaste. Of her, he was the most proud, because other men of the village had not been so diligent or perhaps so lucky.

There were stories of other girls who had been spirited away at night, shrouded and hooded, to a certain doctor who, for a fee, would correct their improprieties. This doctor was known for his discretion, but the village was small and people are cruel, and so the tales that were created to fill the gap in the stories were always much worse than the truth of the matter. So the gossip was spread, and many fathers were forced to send their daughters far away to work, indentured, elsewhere. This was always heartbreaking, for the village would always remember the girls as innocent children, and the families were always close and tightly bound, but to allow even one girl to remain in the village after she had sinned would bring shame to the whole community and could bring the wrath of Heaven upon them. Corrina's father *was* most pleased with her, and he felt safe in the knowledge that she would never bring him to that tearful goodbye that so many of the other men of the village had been forced to endure. He felt safe in the knowledge that she was sleeping peacefully in her bed, in the room next to his.

At the moment though, she was walking barefoot through the dew-laced grass around the edge of the field that had, until now, been the limits of her world. She began to search the darkness of the forest for signs of the tinsel wings of the Faerie people, seeking the outline of the trees in the darkness. The darkness frightened her and she would never have ventured so deeply into the woods at night, had she not been guided by the glow of fairy wings. She thought that she saw something, and was startled and frozen. For a moment, the image of the man, Sitri, flashed in her mind's eye and she thrust the image away in disgust. But then she found herself studying a shadow deep in the woods that faintly resembled him. Was that he? Was he here, outside her window? She turned to flee, to return to her home and wake her father. He would bring the dogs and some of his men and they would hunt the scoundrel to exhaustion, but instead she held fast. She turned back to the shadow and studied it more intently, had it moved? She had never stepped into the forest without the softly glowing light of her Faerie escort, the very thought of it terrified her, but she found herself drawn toward the shadow as it slowly pulled away. Her unshod foot stepped timidly into the edge of the wood and she drew in her breath and followed. The shadow darted just beyond the limits of her vision and faded into the recesses between the trees. She pushed deeper into the dark, hugging herself to keep calm and telling herself that she was unafraid. The memory of Sitri's face returned to her mind and again she forced it down, away from her thoughts. She felt the same as she had before she had slept in the clearing, when she had danced with the stranger who had been spying on her in the woods. She felt as though she was not in her body, not in her own mind. The strange silhouettes of the gnarled tree branches crowded the edges of her vision and scratched at her face and clothes, yet she continued on, undaunted. Why was she out of her bed, why was she pursuing the shadow of the stranger? She did not know. The memory pulled her deeper into the forest. She arrived at the place where she had first glimpsed the shadow and she realized that it had only been the edge of a broken tree. Before she was able to think otherwise, she felt the bitter sensation of disappointment. Why was she feeling this way? Confused and frightened, she went on. There were more shadows and more disappointments as the panic stricken maiden was carried deeper and deeper into the darkness. With tears streaming down her scratched face, she stumbled and nearly fell upon a rocky expanse of ground. She felt as though she could go no further, not because of a physical need for rest but because of a miserable bewilderment. She crumpled to her knees like a wilted flower and there she lay sobbing. She realized that she was terribly lost and that she was helpless without the usual companions that would always light her way home. She felt that she knew the reason that they were not with her on this night. The guilt that she felt because her mind drifted back to the stranger was the reason she was alone. She knew that she should not be in the wood uninvited as surely as a child knows when it has done something wrong and is awaiting punishment. Corrina knew that the Faerie would dance with her no longer. She heard a sound through the choking of her sobs and looked up, wincing as she wiped the tears from her torn cheek. Before her stood Sitri and, as he saw the tears pouring from her eyes, he rushed to kneel at her side. Cradling her in his arms, he kissed away the muddy stains on her cheeks and pulled her chin upward so that she looked directly at him.

"Why are you out here away from your bed?" he asked, glancing beyond her, ever alert to the dangers in the wood. "What would cause you to lose your way so completely?" He brushed a wayward strand of golden hair away from her eyes.

"I was seeking you..." she stammered and tried to pull away from his grasp, but this time he would not release her. She struggled and then, weakly, she surrendered and folded to him. "I saw you near our field, near our home."

"I was not near your home tonight, nor any other night," he replied. "I only just now arrived in these woods. In truth, I was rather lucky that I found you." She began to regain her composure and to return to her usual grace and courage. She made an attempt to smooth her hair and to wipe her eyes and to conceal her emotions but her relief at seeing him was palpable. She felt happier than she had ever felt and she could not comprehend why. He started to help her to her feet but she pulled him closer to the forest floor and so he sat on the ground next to her. "Do you not wish to return to your home? I think I can find the way that you came; I'm quite good at following a trail," he said.

"Not just now," she replied, wrapping her arms around her knees. "I wish to clear my head a little. I'm not quite sure why I came to the wood at all." She rested her forehead on her knees and leaned against him. "I knew that you would seek and find me, just as I knew that I would find you. I just don't know how I knew. It all seems so... *distant.*"

She cast a bewildered glance toward him and as she did, her eye caught the flash of the strange talisman that hung suspended from a chain around his neck. Entranced, she stretched out her hand to reach for it, the mysterious symbols capturing and holding her attention. Sitri pulled away, keeping the stone just beyond her reach, wondering at the same instant what would cause him to do such a thing. She looked up at him sharply and attempted again to grasp the stone and when he again moved away, her temper flared. "What is that around your neck? May I see it more closely?" She was able to cover the impatience in her voice but Sitri knew what the stone was and was certain that her tone just barely concealed her true desire. He knew that the charm was calling out to her, entreating her to cling to it, to him, and he suddenly and inexplicably did not want her near it. It made no sense, his mind was reeling and swaying in a disoriented tumult, for whenever Corrina's hand came close to the stone, he could not force himself to allow her to touch it. Try as she might, she could not get her hand around it. The demon twisted and turned to escape her as she lunged wildly at the charm until finally, her face flushed and red with anger, she stood and stamped her feet in rage. Her expression was one of uncontained fury as she breathlessly glared at the demon before her. "Why won't you give it to me!" she exclaimed, "You said that you would give me the world!"

He replied before he realized what he was saying. "Corrina my love, I cannot give you this charm. I can never allow you to touch it. Nor can I explain to you the reason this is so. Please forget it, and forgive me." They stood face to face in the scattered beams of moonlight, the shadows growing longer around them.

THE TWO DEMON-WIZARDS peered into the crystal ball and viewed the scene in the forest with appraising eyes. The tension that stretched between the two figures that stood in the center was visible as a glowing red band that bound them together. The wizards knew that it was an immensely strong magical power that they were witnessing and that it was made of pure, unadulterated will. Only one of the wizards knew the origin of such power and he smiled inwardly as he watched the drama that he had orchestrated play out inside the crystal.

After a time, Andras addressed him. "Berith, what was the charm that you gave to Sitri? It was no love fetish, of that I am certain. The trap is set and the poison is swallowed. Tell me the truth of the anchor." Andras returned his attention to the two frozen in time in the tiny forest scene within the ball. They still had not moved. Berith studied the band extending from Corrina to Sitri and made a pronouncement formed from a practiced eye.

"Do you see how the tie that binds them is a pure light, Andras? Do you see the girth of it, the strength of it? That is because of the purity of the girl." He continued to expound on the subject like an academic, a professor in a lecture hall. "The fact that Sitri is ignorant of the gift that he wears is strengthening it as well." He shifted his gaze to a better angle and went on, "They will both play into our hands in time, and nature must play its course."

But Andras was not to be put off. "What was the charm, Berith? How have you twisted the plan? What flavor of evil have you seasoned this with? I must know." He waited expectantly for Berith to finish his inspection.

The duke finally raised his head from the ball and spoke. "You are correct, Andras. It was most certainly not a love charm. The anchor is far more powerful than a mere trinket such as that. The fool Sitri has no idea what it is that he wears around his idiot neck. You must wait to find out as well, for wickedness is so much sweeter when practiced in secret. Watch and learn, my fallen comrade, watch and learn." He turned back to the crystal ball.

In the forest, Sitri was reeling from the sensations that were coursing through him. He reached for Corrina and was unable to force himself to close the distance between them. There was a churning in his guts that nearly threw him to his knees and a continuous roaring and buzzing in his skull. He could not express it, even within himself, yet the feeling was vaguely familiar to him, a hallucination that was experienced by a person asleep and dreaming. He wanted the girl, but he could not touch her. Corrina had looked past the charm that hung from Sitri's neck and saw him instead. Her eyes moistened again but this time with excitement and joy and she moved to embrace him. She saw with clear eyes now and realized why she had crossed the threshold of the forest edge. She saw why she had sought the stranger who had danced with her in the glade in the forest. She knew that she loved him and needed him to love her in return. As she moved to embrace him, he recoiled from her, stepping backward and stumbling in his haste to stay away. An expression of pain and confusion flashed across her face and yet she was undaunted and she tried again. Again he stepped back. Anger and frustration filled her countenance, her shoulders dropped and her eyes welled with hot tears.

"Why are you running from me?" she exclaimed. "Why won't you take me?" She crumpled to the forest floor, unable to face him. Stifled sobs arose from her as she buried her face in her hands and wept. Perplexed, Sitri stood over her and felt the strange and mysterious thoughts form in his mind. He looked down upon her and felt...*compassion*. He was mystified. What had happened to him? What was happening to him? He did not know, but he knew that he should comfort the young girl who had wandered lost into a strange wood, and had entrusted herself to his charge. He bent, and found that he could approach and touch her. He tucked the stone away so that it would not brush against her skin and bundled her, sobbing, into his arms. He started off, through the forest, following the path that she had broken between the underbrush. After a time, she slept and he strode through the twilight, brooding about the parcel that he carried. He saw the lights of a farmhouse and knew that it was the place that she had come from and then, silently and peacefully, as only an angel could, he replaced her in her bed.

Chapter 5

Punishment

SITRI sat cross-legged in a mournful pose, his head bent. He was positioned in the center of the clearing in the forest where he had first encountered Corrina. The air was thick and hot, a sticky film of hazy fog was swirling about the ferns and the clover. He was awaiting his judgment, steeling himself for the punishment that he knew was his final due. A pall was settling over the forest, as though the trees themselves were casting their votes against him, and he felt the oppressive gloom acutely. It did not take long before the first of the jury arrived. A pair of shadowy forms began to manifest from the wisps of vapor that floated across the glade, slowly materializing into the Ministers, Berith and Andras.

"Where is the girl, Sitri? What have you done with her? Our lord wished that she remain with you until the moment of his arrival. He always prefers to announce his claim personally and immediately. You know that." Andras stepped forward from the mist that wrapped around his feet and looked around the clearing. "You were to keep her alive and healthy. Is she restrained somewhere nearby?" He glanced at the other wizard who was stepping out of the haze as well, seeking a hint in the eyes of the senior wizard. He looked for any sign of trickery, impatient for the duke to reveal the truth behind the trap that he had laid. Berith's eyes were impassive, his expression a perfect mask of innocence.

He moved toward Sitri and spoke. "Our master will be here soon, Sitri. Now is not the time for such a sullen face. He will be delighted with your work, as always. Come now, let us see this perfect maiden who was pure enough to attract the sight of the Crown Prince of Hell himself." There was a tinge of darkness in the duke's voice, a foreshadowing of the terrors to come. Sitri looked up at the two sorcerers, seeing for the first time the filth and stink that they were draped in. Before, they had appeared as elder statesman, adorned in the dignified trappings of the court, but now their ancient armor was rusted and caked in blood and slime, and their exposed skin flaked away beneath it. He recoiled from the sight, confused and shaken.

"What is it that you are wearing? What trickery is this?" He fell back on the heels of his hands and pulled himself away. The Ministers were standing before him, arrayed in their true form. He finally saw them for what they really were, and with shock he realized that he appeared that way as well. He was horrified and fascinated all at once. The fallen angels were surrounded on all sides by an aureole of darkness, a sort of negative corona that swallowed the sunlight and reflected nothing. A sensation of sorrow and anger emanated from the halo as though it was itself alive, and Sitri knew that in a way, it was. He saw himself inside the shroud and realized suddenly that he was able to witness it because he was actually outside of it, looking in. The Ministers were not made of flesh or bone, but of the shape of wickedness. There was an asymmetry to their form that reached deep into their interiors and extended out beyond to touch the trees. Even the trees seemed to shy away from the ugliness and were amazingly beautiful by comparison. Sitri felt a tearing in his center as he became aware that he himself was made in the same way. His sorrow was complete. He struggled to pick himself up from the forest floor but was rendered immobile by his shame and the Ministers moved closer to him.

"Where is the girl, Sitri?" whispered Berith into his ear. He leaned in so that his breath was rasping and coarse. "Time is short now, we must know where she is. Unless of course, you do not have her here. Why in all the worlds would she not be in your possession? Especially with all of the help that we have given you." Andras saw the gleam in Berith's eye and knew that the duke was about to reveal his treachery. He had been a part of many of Berith's iniquities and could sense when he had tired of the game. Andras moved close to Sitri so that he too could enjoy the springing of the snare. Berith's face contorted into a grimace of smug pleasure, he licked his lips as if to actually taste and relish Sitri's failure. "Tell us about Corrina, tell us about your courtship."

"Get away from me!" exclaimed Sitri. "I do not know how you have deceived me Berith, but I will revenge it." He attempted to rise but was held in place by the sudden weight of the stone around his neck. Berith laughed aloud.

"Do you feel it, Sitri? The talisman that I gave you? No love charm for the great Sitri, no." He wrapped a claw of a hand around the stone and studied the glyphs that were carved into it. "This is an anchor, a lodestone if you will. I can see that you feel its weight. It was instrumental in our descent. From the time after The Litany of Stars." He saw the rage in Sitri's face. "You don't remember do you, Sitri. Such a pity that you do not share my appreciation of the history of our race." He snapped the chain that tied the stone to Sitri's neck and returned the Anchor to the depths of his robe. "It was not so very long ago after all, that we were all as you are now." He leaned even closer and whispered ever so gently to the soldier between them. "The stone makes you a mortal man." Before Sitri could react, the very air above them began to tear and shimmer. A reddish glow came over all the forest and the mist turned to vapor and then began to steam. The dark prince appeared, seated on his throne in the center of the clearing. Both demon wizards turned to face their master and bowed low on one knee.

With their eyes still on the ground, they spoke as one voice. "Hail, Lord Prince and greetings, we have only just arrived and wish to know your command." The prince nodded in acquiescence and blinked to acknowledge his ministers. He took in the scene before him and narrowed his eyes.

After a moment, he spoke. "Sitri, arise." The prince's voice was pitiless and cold. His gaze bore down on the figure kneeling before him and waited for him to stand. When Sitri had risen to his feet and had raised his head to look upon the prince, the prince gestured to him to approach. When Sitri was near enough to the throne, the prince reached out and grasped him by the chin. Turning and examining both sides of the face in his hand, the prince paused for a moment and then spoke. "This is a mortal that stands before me, how has this come to pass?" The two demons that waited behind Sitri remained kneeling silently on the forest floor. The prince let go of Sitri's chin and clenched his teeth, great sinews stood out on his copper neck. "HOW HAS THIS COME TO PASS?" he roared. He looked through and beyond the man who stood in front of him and his eyes bored into the kneeling wizards. "Explain this, Berith."

The minister rose to his feet and slowly approached the throne. He glared viciously at Sitri as he walked forward and turned his hate filled eyes toward his master. He halted when he was still a few steps away and spoke in a grating voice. "I used an anchor, my Lord. A relic of the Fall. It was to translate Sitri to mortal flesh for a time. He is mortal still and will remain for some time." He finished and stepped back.

The prince fixed an icy gaze upon him and spoke again. "Did you know of this, Andras?" he questioned.

Andras glanced upwards and spoke truthfully. "No, Sire, I knew nothing of the stone." He only moved to address the prince and then returned his attention to the ground.

The prince focused once more on Sitri, and his tone was menacing. "Where is the girl?" he asked.

Sitri stood solidly and spoke boldly. "I left her in her home with her father." His demeanor was resolute. He still was mystified as to how he had arrived at the state he was in. He had no idea what it meant to be mortal but he was certain that showing fear before the prince would do him no good. The prince had no mercy and had never shown any consideration for cowardice. Many before Sitri had begged and pleaded for it but none had yet received it, so Sitri stood his ground and spoke plainly, "I did not violate her as you wished."

The prince regarded both Sitri and Berith with a barely contained fury; he appeared to be pondering the manner in which he would destroy them. Then without warning, he clapped his hands and the glade in the forest was empty and silent, save for the twittering of the goldfinches and squirrels that played in the morning sun.

They reappeared in the prince's chamber, standing before him in his court of tin, copper and bronze. The prince was in the same form as before, copper-skinned and goat-horned and he stared into the pool of liquid fire and regarded things of the past and of things yet to come and things of this very instant. He beckoned for the others to come and look into the pool, and they saw that it was there that they would receive their judgment. All three edged the pool on the opposite side of the prince and peered through the flames at the scene contained within it. They saw Corrina's little village and they saw a small group of villagers gathered together near a shrouded and hooded figure. The figure wore a veil, yet even through the lace Sitri could see the features of Corrina. He faltered and reached out to put his hand into the flame when he was held back by the voice of the prince.

"Hold, Sitri. Do you not know what it is that you see? What do you believe is held within the scrying pool?" The prince shifted in the throne, resting his chin on his hand and resting his elbow on the top of his leg. "What is it that you reach for?" Sitri could not take his eyes from the vision in the pool; the others around her, who were weeping inconsolably and tearing at their clothes, embraced Corrina's shrouded figure. One man in particular was more distraught than the others; he had to be pulled away from the maiden as she was bundled into a coach, where the shades on the windows were quickly drawn. The man fell to his knees, his face buried in his hands as the coach pulled slowly away from the assembled people.

Sitri spoke in a low voice. "I see the girl being removed for her own good, to keep her away from us and our kind." He paused, and then went on, "She is pure and they will send her to the Abbey. She will be a nun." He watched as the people tried to comfort the stricken father, but he lashed out at them in a rage. The tiny crowd finally left him, sobbing, in the lane.

The prince's voice became more sinister. "No Sitri, that is not what is in the pool. Tell me, truthfully, how do you feel about the girl. Hold nothing back from me, for I will know and it will be worse for you if you do." He sat back and clasped his hands together. Sitri finally took his eyes from the pool.

"I love her dearly," he replied. "She is worth any punishment. I would protect her from the miseries of Hell for eternity if I could, but I will not have to. She is out of your reach now." He looked stoically into the eyes of the devil and set his jaw. "She is safe from us," he finished.

The prince leaned his head back and released a long, wicked laugh, the noise of it causing the whole of the chamber to tremble. Berith cringed. "No, Sitri, you are mistaken. She goes not to the convent but to the surgeon. She is mine now and forever. Your only chance to protect her was to never abandon her, and when you left her alone and rejected, you left her for me. The heart of a mortal man is stupid and backwards and at its very center, evil. She would have saved you both if only you had allowed her, but now you both are lost. Stand firm for your judgment." He turned his head to his minister. "Berith, you shall be judged as well." He made a motion and a scepter appeared in his left hand. His right formed a sign that traced strange motions in the air above the flames of the pool. The flames themselves danced in crackling obedience to their lord's movements. Both Sitri and Berith resolutely awaited the judgment of Hell.

The prince spoke grimly as his hand wrote in the smoke of the flames. "Berith, thou hast given the Anchor of Flesh to an angel and brought again the stain of the Descent. In thy pride and envy, thou hast rekindled the War and broken the treaty. For this sin that even a demon is forbidden by The Most High, thou shall follow the path of the Anchor to the depths of the Flesh that created it. Even *I* fear the deeper realm, beyond even Hell and Earth. Thou hast cast this enchantment so thou shall carry this stone.

"Sitri, thou shall be cursed. Mortal thou art, and mortal thou shall remain. Thy original sin, though long forgotten, can never be forgiven and thy compassion will forever separate thee from the ranks of Hell. Walk the world within it but never of it, and always be reminded of the tragedy of thy love. Only when the end of days is upon the Earth and the final angel sings The Litany of Stars once more, shall thou be released. This doom is not destined, as our exile is our own free will and if my will be done, that song shall never be sung. Now, be gone from my presence and may there be no mercy for thee."

The Second Tale

The Speaker

Chapter 6

Exile

Alone in the Darkness, a starkness, a bleakness,
A coldness envelops thy heart and thy weakness
is shown in thy shivering, trembling, quivering
terror, the nearer one walks in thy meekness.

Vanished thy Beauty and vanished thy Bloom,
Vanished thy vigor, approacheth thy tomb.
Lonely, forsaken, thy lover has taken
thy grace and in place of it left thee this doom.

One sorrow to pain thee, to chain thee and hideth,
Another that pierceth and wounds and abideth
enshrouding Another, waiting to smother
thy heart, torn apart by deception that guideth

Thine eyes to the faded, thy ears to the still,
Thy tongue to the bitter, Thy touch to the chill
The scent of despair is perfumed everywhere.
Now shattered are scattered the shards of thy will.
It is done...

SITRI FOUND HIMSELF ALONE. The passage of time was once again voided as it was when he had been created and he saw the expansion of the stars and the flowering of man as one instant. The narrow, silvery thread of his identity played out behind him as he was cast into the current of the stream. He heard the music that had once been his birthright and he felt again the envy and anger he had felt when he thought of the blessings of man, yet no sooner had he been touched by this anger than he also felt the immense sorrow and emptiness of space. He remembered the rebellion and wept. Beyond the extremes of dark that washed over him, he spied the others, the ones who had never disobeyed. He saw them burning in the heavens...

Then in the silence, A WORD, a vibration,
A tone in the quiet of thy meditation
arises and slowly caresses thy lowly
spirit, to Hear it in such desolation!

Softly with Beauty, Softly with care,
Softly with patience, the note fills the air.
Steadily swelling and speaking and telling,
New voices to join it and bid thee to hear.

One voice to arouse thee, to wake thee while greeting,
Another that staunches thy wounds that are bleeding.
Embracing and tending the next which is mending
Thy heart of thy heart with compassion and leading

Thine eyes to the sacred, thy touch to the strong,
Thy tongue to the sweetness, thine ears to the song.
A fragrance of rose quickens and grows.
The chorus has sung in the darkness too long.

A spark in the distance, an ember, just glowing,
ignites in the vast depths of dark and starts growing,
erupting and burning, enflaming thy yearning
for being, for seeing, not wishing but knowing.

Knowing the Wisdom and Knowing the Grace.
Knowing the Love which revealed the face
of infinite mirrors reflecting the bearers
of torches and candles all in their place.

One flame to lead thee, a beacon unveiling,
Another that shineth like stars never failing,
spreading and forming the heavens and warming
the chill in thy breast with affection and hailing

Thine eyes for they see, thine ears for they hear,
Thou tasteth the honey and toucheth the sphere
Beyond what deceiveth, thy spirit receiveth
the gifts of the Speaker, who holds thee most dear.

IN THE PLACE that he had once stood he heard them singing. The song had no beginning and no end, it had always been sung and Sitri was outside of it. He sat in the darkness in the deep reaches of space and felt the frigid vastness of it. He prayed in terror, that he would not be abandoned there and that he would still be granted a reprieve. He did not have long to wait.

Chapter 7

The Children

<hr>

*Of a brother and sister
and of a mother's loss*

THE SOLITARY, hooded figure sat cross-legged next to a
dwindling, smoky fire. He leaned closer, as if to embrace what little light and heat it offered. Casting a momentary glance in the direction from which he had come,
he then turned his gaze to the way he would walk at dawn.

His thoughts turned inward and he briefly contemplated the events which, seemingly disconnected, had conspired to bring him to that point. His eyes shifted upward and lingered on the constellations, which splayed across the blackness above. He closed his eyes.

Inward and downward went his thoughts, his breathing slowed ever so slightly. Where he had been, where he was to go, the events of the recent and not so recent past, the flickering fire before him and the stars that pinwheeled across the night. He pondered these things. He relaxed and focused at the same time, a paradoxical skill which had taken him much effort to master. Slowing his breathing yet again, he allowed his mind to settle on one, clear, pure thought: his task, the journey he had been selected and trained for. Slowly, he became aware of where he was. Not simply his location upon the Earth, his elementary training insured that he was continuously aware of that, but a deeper, more intimate location. He referenced his mind to the ever-shifting stars and to the chilling wind which blew from behind him. He felt the soft pull of the moon against the constant tug of the Earth and sensed the throbbing vibration of the sea that was miles to the west of him. He was centered. He remained that way until dawn.

Before the light of the sun crossed the horizon, he felt its warmth. The fire had dwindled hours before and the meager glow of the remaining embers competed with the grayish light of the impending sunrise. The movement of his eyes opening seemed to be the only disturbance in the calm. He waited.

As the first ray of sunlight broke through the cold grayness, he pushed back his hood with both hands and studied his surroundings. Although he had no map, he knew there was a road half a mile from where he sat. It would be the first road that he had walked on in days. Faithful to his training, he preferred to travel on foot, at night, and to avoid roads if possible. While his eyes sought out a potential route toward the road, the sun began to warm him in earnest. He stood and stretched, first his arms straight above his head, inhaling, then bending at the waist, exhaling. He touched his palms to the dirt just beyond his boots, and then straightened. There was nothing so obvious as a path of any sort, but there had been none the whole way. The way was downhill slightly and the vegetation sparse, it had been decreasing through the earlier part of the night. The traveler had built his fire at the periphery of the brush to somewhat conceal himself; although he knew there was no need and that there were no people near him, it was a habit in which he took comfort. He also knew that the first part of his task was nearly complete, for he felt the proximity of his destination. He knew that he would encounter people soon and sighed. He had traveled in the bush for over a week now, moving slowly and methodically at night, and today he would walk in daylight and on a man-made road, his task required it. He picked up his pack, pulled his hood up and started off.

SOLOMON WORTH was eight years old and deeply troubled. He was troubled because his little sister was dying and it didn't bother him. Troubled because his mother hated him and it didn't bother him. Troubled because they were so poor and none of it bothered him. His father had named him Solomon after a king in the Bible and then he'd died and Solomon Worth had never cared. He had never known his father except through stories his mother had told him and, because of those stories, he felt relieved that he had never known him. His mother had always struggled, always worked, always cried at night for as long as he could remember and he had always known that everyone, eventually, dies. Solomon, his mother, and his sick sister, Mara, had moved out into the middle of nowhere when Mara got worse. For a while she had gotten better and it seemed like things were going to be okay, but the last time she got worse, his mother had taken him out of school and everything had changed. She had quit her job, made them move out there in the woods and just stayed home with Mara. Solomon had missed the entire second grade and was missing the third, too. His mother hadn't spoken to him since the night she hit him. He had gotten angry and said that he couldn't wait for Mara to die, because then they could move back and have money again. Then she hit him. Hard. After that, she walked into Mara's room, the room that always stank and locked him out. Solomon had meant what he said, he knew Mara wasn't going to get better, and he knew that she hurt all the time. Why couldn't girls be tough like him? He spent the days outside the gray clapboard house, in the woods, thinking. He only went inside to make himself lunch and to sleep at night. He snuck in. He hated it in there. He missed his mother and Mara terribly, but he knew that they were never coming back, just like his father was never coming back. Every day he wanted to run away, but he was much too frightened. There was only one dirt road leading to the little house and there was nothing on it. Solomon walked down it a little further each day, hoping to see the house they had passed when they moved there, but it was further than he remembered.

Today was the worst day yet. In the mornings, he would wait until he heard his mother preparing breakfast for herself and the door to Mara's room open and shut; he would then creep downstairs and outside through the kitchen door. He was always hungry and it was always cold that early but he didn't care about that either. He could wait until lunch, it was better than facing his mother. His mother had stopped making food for Mara because Mara had stopped eating. After that, his mother had stopped eating lunch and stayed in the room all day. When his hunger became too great to bear, he would tiptoe silently up the gray wooden stairs to the kitchen door, slide inside and quietly steal food. Today, his mother had caught him.

Solomon froze. He stared wide-eyed at his mother who was framed in the doorway leading to the kitchen; his hand was riveted to the handle of the refrigerator door. He saw little Mara in his mother's face and he knew that he looked like them as well, the same dark eyes, the same dark, straight hair. Mara's face was always soft, serene, and even when she was in such pain, she was never angry. But his mother's face reflected his hardness and bitterness. Both Solomon and his mother were always angry now. For one brief flash, Solomon perceived a softening of his mother's features, a tenderness that he hadn't seen in a long time. And then it was gone, replaced by a cold, granite stare. He subconsciously realized that it wasn't tenderness, it was sorrow and despair and he knew then that his little sister was going to die, today. His mother moved suddenly and he recoiled as if burned but she simply looked through him and sat at the kitchen table. He stood still, afraid to speak, to breathe. She lowered her face into her hands and began to sob softly. Solomon walked outside, stood next to her car and listened to her weeping.

MARA LAY IN HER BED and held Brownie tightly in her arms. She heard Solomon go outside and heard her mother crying. She knew that when she cried it sometimes made her mother cry. She tried not to cry at all, or to cover her face with Brownie if she felt tears. Sometimes she couldn't help it, and she would bury her face in Brownie's soft fur and feel the paw with no fur rub her ear. The paw that she used to suck on when she was a baby. Now, she was too tired to bring Brownie to her face, she was too tired to cry. She wondered why Solomon didn't come to see her or play with her anymore, why he didn't like her anymore. She knew that he was outside, next to the car. She always knew where he was, down the hall from her in his room or outside walking on the road, even though she couldn't see him, and she wished he would come and sit next to her, like he did when she first got sick. He never cried. He acted like she wasn't even sick, just tired, and it made her feel like she was getting better. She heard the car door open and slam shut and heard the car start and, for a moment, she thought that her mother had left her, but then she knew that it was Solomon. She could still hear her mother crying in the kitchen. She squeezed Brownie a little tighter and smiled. He was going to get in so much trouble when Mom found out.

THE HOODED MAN LOOKED AHEAD, down the dirt road, and saw the small, gray car lodged unevenly in the shallow ravine that edged it. He halted, adjusting his pack straps, and listened to the engine idling softly in the distance. He had wished not to be seen but this was a road, cars were to be expected. He resumed his approach. As he drew near, he glimpsed through the windshield a small, dark-haired boy behind the steering wheel. The boy's tear stained face darted anxiously about but he had not yet noticed the figure walking towards him. His face dropped out of sight for a moment and the engine raced. The man smiled slightly. The boy was too small to see while he was driving and had slid into the muddy ravine. One wheel sprayed mud to the rear of the car and it shifted even deeper into the ditch. When the boy resurfaced, he gasped sharply, startled to see a man through the dusty glass of the windshield. The man slid back his hood, leaned gently forward, looked into the boy's terrified eyes and spoke.

"Child, why do you cry?" The man's voice was not un-friendly, but Solomon cringed sharply away from its sound. The sudden appearance of the man overwhelmed him and he nearly choked on his breath. The stranger spoke again. "You don't seem like the sort to cry." It was not said as en-couragement. He spoke plainly and sincerely, it was simple observed fact. Solomon never cried. He hated when people cried.

"I'm not crying!" he reacted. "Only girls cry!" Then, like a lidded pot suddenly boiling over, he burst into tears.

"True indeed, child, but I'll not tell if you won't. Be calm and whatever the cause, we'll fix it." With his hand still extended, the stranger smiled, just a bit. Solomon, almost imperceptibly, softened.

"You can't fix it. No one can fix it," he sobbed.

"Boy, be calm!" The stranger's voice had changed, be-come larger. Solomon stopped crying. Suddenly, he felt no panic or sorrow, no loneliness or desperation. It was as though the stranger's voice wrapped around him like a blanket and the sadness of the day was outside of it. The stranger continued to beckon to him. "We will fix it," he said.

SOLOMON FOUND HIMSELF on the dirt road leading back to Mara and his mother. He followed a few paces behind the stranger as a queer sort of numbness settled behind his eyes. The car remained in the ravine, abandoned. Although the stranger's pace was steady and strong, even for a man, the boy seemed to match it with little effort. He felt like something was pulling him in the stranger's wake, something real and physical. A gentle, yet firm and actual tugging from the stranger that seemed to center on a spot between his heart and his belly drew him forward. Solomon was neither frightened nor tired, nor was he curious, he simply studied the stranger's grayish leather boots as he trudged in his footprints, two steps for every one the stranger took. From the moment the man had commanded him to be calm, he had felt a strange peace wash over him. His eight-year-old heart had been broken and his eight-year-old mind knew nothing of that, so he simply let the invisible blanket of the stranger's voice comfort and warm him. They fell into a rhythm, two steps for every one. Presently they came upon the desolate gray house.

MARA HEARD the kitchen door open; she felt the suction pull her bedroom door against its frame. She felt Solomon enter the kitchen with somebody new and she heard her mother speaking to them and then, Mara died.

When she was still a baby, before she could talk, her mother would bring her and her brother to the beach. Solomon would grasp her hand and pull her, toddling, toward the surf and she knew that the salty, murmuring throb of the waves was the same as the pulse inside of her. Deep in her chest and deep in her ear was the same murmur, the same throb and so she was never afraid. Solomon held her in the shallows, and there she floated, smiling a baby's smile, looking at the sun, in between the sky and the earth.

Now, in her bedroom, she felt the pulse in her heart and in her head again. She could hear the whispering of the ocean, just like at the beach, but now she could hear words in the waves. The waves were singing to her, just a little too quietly to be heard clearly. It was the prettiest song Mara could remember hearing and, sitting up straight to listen, she forgot her weariness and tilted her head like a puppy in wonder. Her mother was still speaking to the new person in the kitchen but those weren't the words in her ear.

She could see the sun above her in her bedroom, just past the Playskool mobile that hung from the ceiling and the sun was singing too, warmer and deeper than the waves, but just as quietly. Mara set Brownie beside her and closed her eyes, stretched her arms out and lifted her chin, letting the glow from the sun make a reddish haze of her eyelids. The waves held her with a swaying motion that rocked her in time with their song, and she could almost smell the salt and the sand. When she opened her eyes, she was standing at the foot of her bed.

SOLOMON'S MOTHER awoke with a start. She raised her tear-soaked eyes to see a man seating himself at her kitchen table, dressed from head to toe in gray. His clothing was not unusual, apart from the uniformity of its dusty, gray hue. He wore a rough pullover shirt that was hooded like an athletic sweatshirt, yet the word that appeared in her mind was "tunic". The rather large hood was up, surrounding his face and hiding the details of his hair and ears. He sat noiselessly and clasped his hands on the table between them. Just beyond him stood her son, his face flushed with exertion, his black hair unkempt, his eyes fixed on the hooded man. The surrealism of the moment was complete. The sheer impossibility of it triggered a dream-like, slow motion reaction in the grief-stricken woman, and she blinked very slowly and shuddered. A sensation, like nausea, vibrated through her, then quickly passed and, laboriously, she began to form a thought.

"Don't ask me who I am," interjected the stranger softly. "You won't understand or believe me."

The tone of his voice cut her thought in two. Who he was and how he was here fell to the bottom of her mind, the question was replaced by fear. Fear for Solomon, her sole remaining child, fear for herself and finally, fear for Mara. At this last thought, a gaping, raw wound opened in her heart, swallowing the fear and spitting up anger. She shuddered again and began to shake violently. Her eyes narrowed to black slits and she surged to lash out at the man opposite her. He held up a hand.

"Be at peace," he said.

Tranquility. . .

Serenity. . .

Peace.

It was as if the stranger's hand had caught her like a fragile, delicate toy, she could not remember feeling such safety and comfort since she was an infant. Her shoulders slumped; she sat back in her chair, her eyes softening and moistening as her lips parted in awe. Many months of terror and sadness, months of pity and false hopes, months and months of rage and confusion wrapped so tightly in one woman's heart, all ending on one single day. A trance-like expression spread across her face.

"Who are you?" she whispered.

"I told you, you won't understand or believe me," replied the stranger. "I've come for the child."

A dim spark of realization flickered in her eyes. Slowly, inexorably, awareness welled up in her. "I know who you are. . ." she choked, "you—"

"No.   You do not," interrupted the stranger firmly. "Please, I must see her now." He rose to his feet, sliding the chair silently across the linoleum. Solomon, his eyes shifting in a daze from the stranger to his mother, pointed limply to Mara's door. He watched, in a dream, as his mother raised her hand to her forehead and made a crossing sign over her chest. He had never seen her do that before, and it had a stunning effect on him. He felt as if he was glued to the floor and his arm held suspended by wires from the ceiling. He held this pose as the stranger walked toward Mara's bedroom, turned the doorknob and opened the door.

Chapter 8

Death and Life

Of the death of a child
and of celestial song

MARA heard the doorknob turn and heard the scrape and click of the latch. She could feel the new person on the other side of the door and sensed his entrance and she knew what he would look like before she saw him. It was like how they always drew the bad guys in cartoons or the super-heroes in comic books. The gray man with the hood just seemed like the man who should walk into her room when the sun and the waves were singing. He was like someone from a story her mother had read to her a long time ago, so long ago she couldn't remember imagining him. She remembered him now, though. He opened the door and stepped into her bedroom with Solomon and her mother behind him and she saw that he heard the singing too; his mouth went right along with the words. He knew the song! Mara wished she could sing it but she couldn't make it out. She started to smile and jump up and down but she felt stuck as though her feet were sticky. It felt spooky and scared her a little bit but the gray man looked at her at the foot of the bed and smiled. Then he winked and she felt okay. She suddenly noticed two things at once: she realized that all the parts inside her didn't hurt anymore, and, at the same time, she saw another little girl in her bed! Holding Brownie! She tried to move toward her bear but the sticky feeling was still there. The gray man smiled at her again, knelt next to her bed, and folded his hands. He had a big, gray backpack on, a lot bigger than her Dora backpack. He closed his eyes and kept singing the song in a whisper. Even when he smiled at her he never stopped whispering the song. The waves were still gently rocking her and the sun was still shining from her bedroom ceiling, she looked up at the warm sun and saw that she didn't have to squinch her eyes like at the beach. The song sounded like it was louder and clearer near the sun. Mara wanted to climb up on her bed so that she could hear the words better, but as soon as she thought that, the gray man opened his eyes, glancing sharply and her and sternly shaking his head. No. Mara knew that he meant "NO", like when her mother told her to wait for her soup to cool. She looked back at Brownie, and saw both Solomon and her mother looking at the other little girl. The other girl was still, like an old porcelain doll and her eyes never closed, and, although Mara thought she was ugly and scary, her mother was looking at her like she was very beautiful. Mara wondered where the other girl had come from and wondered why neither her mother nor brother was looking at her. Confused, frightened, and slightly angry, Mara forgot the song and the sun and the waves and reached for her brother.

The very instant that she thought of Solomon, her feet lost that stickiness. She drifted in the current closer to him and her tiny hand brushed his. The moment that she touched it, there was a small blue snap of static and another hand appeared. Solomon's left hand seemed to mirror itself, then his wrist, and then his elbow. Another crack of electricity and there was a second Solomon standing beside the first, astounded at the vision of his sister standing on her own. Looking wildly about, he took in the scene arrayed before him in amazement. His invalid sister seemed to be alive and walking (a feat which she had been unable to perform for over a year), while her lifeless body continued to adorn her bed. He saw himself staring down at her, gaping dumbly at her stiffened arms as they clutched a tattered, stuffed bear. He watched as the kneeling stranger lifted his eyes from the small form lying prone before him, and looked up at the apparition of Mara that had touched his hand. Then, finally the stranger's gaze settled firmly on Solomon. The boy was startled at this somehow. He saw that his mother, just behind the stranger, was oblivious to the walking Mara. Solomon knew that, had she seen Mara up, she would have rushed to embrace her. Instead, she remained focused on the cold figure of her daughter in her accustomed place. As though responding to a question that Solomon had not yet created, the stranger's eyes held his attention.

She cannot see us.

I can see you both.

Help me fix Mara.

Unspoken and not conceived yet. Thoughts that were not yet thoughts, simply hopes and memories, flashed between the three of them.

Help fix me, Solomon.

Mom can't see us.

Listen to the song, Solomon.

The stranger was whispering words that Solomon couldn't understand. He had thought that the gray man had been on his knees praying, but now he heard music accompanying him and, just slightly, at the corners of his hearing, he heard a song. When he looked at the stranger's lips, he could see that they fit the music and he could vaguely make out other voices singing, but he could not hear the words. He tried, but they were too distant.

Not with your ears, Solomon.

Watch me sing.

Solomon stared intensely at the lips as they moved in a stilted cadence; he watched the song as it formed. As he watched, a sense of déjà vu grew in his mind. The song seemed familiar, an ancient nursery rhyme with a sad ending, or perhaps an old folk song that he knew from the times of his earliest memories. His own lips began to move with the stranger's, reciting of their own accord, a song that he had never known. The other Solomon started singing as well, whispering under his breath, his lips moving in unison with the man kneeling by the bed. With an astonished intake of breath, Solomon's mother snapped her head up to look at him. Her son's eyes were empty, hollow. He folded his hands together, mimicking the stranger. She realized abruptly that she was totally alone in the bedroom. The solitude was a tangible thing, a sudden vacancy that permeated the room. Solomon and the stranger were moving but they were not there with her. Of that she was certain. A creeping desolation slowly enveloped her as she listened, horrified, to the rustling of the silent singing.

Solomon, teach Mara the words.

Beyond understanding, Solomon obeyed, his left hand groping for Mara's right.

Teach me the words, Solomon.

He saw Mara reaching for the second time; he saw the vision of himself, hands clasped stiffly, like a puppet. He saw the stranger singing, eyes closed now, concentrating, and he saw his mother, unaware of the real Mara, unaware of him.

Teach me the words.

Please.

The hands of the children locked together. Mara smiled, her eyes laughing.

A thousand memories came flooding in. All of the days in the sunlight, before the world was gray. The children remembered the time before memory, before it was possible to forget and their eyes opened wider than the sun or the ocean. The words of the song were clear now, perfectly clear and understandable. Each syllable of the continuous flow was bell-like and articulate. More than that, every word could be felt and seen. The children felt the song in their heads and bellies, in their spines and feet and they saw the music as each distinct melody manifested into shimmering color, as the harmony wove itself into a fabric of warm light. They had been here before. This was their song. Mara picked up the lyric at the precise moment that her part began, singing a melody that fit elegantly into the infinite musical pattern. Her lilting voice lifted the energy of the song noticeably, and the words themselves announced her return.

Mara, you cannot stay.

Amidst the vibrating shower of light, she looked down and saw her brother's hand in hers. She looked up into his face.

I haven't died yet.

The children's mother heard a faint noise below her. Stricken with awe, she glanced down at the face of her departed daughter and imagined a slight movement there. Did it seem like a vague flush of color on Mara's lips? A yearning flutter kicked deep within the mother's chest. Were her lips moving? Her cheeks blushing? As color washed into the little girl's face, it was as if life flowed into the mother's heart as well. She reached over the stranger's shoulder and squeezed the cold hand that held the toy bear. The hand squeezed in reply. Gasping, she leaned closer to Mara and heard a breathy whisper emanating from her; she saw her lips moving in sync with the stranger's. She felt warmth and strength in her daughter's hand, strength that she hadn't had that morning, strength that she hadn't had in months. With a sucking sound, Mara took in a sudden whooshing breath; she blinked and licked her lips. Her mother felt the presence of both the stranger and Solomon in the bedroom with her. Solomon dropped his hands and rushed to wrap his arms around his sister. Mara looked up at her mother's hopeful face.

"Mommy, I'm hungry," she said.

She fell upon her daughter, sobbing through the laughter, lifting her from the pillow and smothering her with kisses. Mara, smiling, looked over her mother's shoulder at the strange man in her bedroom. He opened his eyes, unclasped his hands and swept a bead of perspiration from his forehead. Rising to his feet, he shifted the weight of his pack on his shoulders, and smiled at the dark-haired child.

"Welcome back, Mara," he said.

IN THE KITCHEN of the small, gray house, a mother busily prepared breakfast for her children and guest. She had spent a sleepless night, sneaking into Mara's room every fifteen minutes or so, checking on her peaceful rest. Each time that she entered, Solomon would be waiting for her, sitting on the edge of his sister's bed, holding her hand. He seldom slept through the night anyway. After the miraculous events of the last evening, the stranger had taken off his backpack and wordlessly walked to the living room. There he dropped his pack and settled, cross-legged on the floor in the front of her couch. He hadn't moved or made a sound since. He made her incredibly nervous, perhaps more nervous than she had ever been.

What had happened last night? What had he done to Mara? What had he done to all of them? She was afraid to ask, even if only to ask herself. What if he took away the gift he had given, what if it had been a dream? As she cracked eggs into a pan, she shook her head, as if to shake away that notion. It wasn't a dream, Mara was alive. She had been dead. Dead. The man was still there, barely breathing, sitting on her living room floor. Her memory of his arrival was hazy, it was a speeded-up film in her mind. First, the gray man at her table, then, him on his knees praying for Mara. After that, her holding Mara until she fell asleep in her arms, even though Mara had wanted to run and play. She had been afraid to let her go.

As she spun between the kitchen counter, coffee maker and the stove-top, she stopped suddenly. A noise was coming from Mara's room, a loud banging. In a panic, she flew around the table toward the bedroom, tears already welling in her eyes. She jerked open the door and burst in. Solomon and Mara were bouncing in tandem on the bed, the headboard clacking loudly into the wall. Mara was the more focused of the two, a determined frown on her face, since she had to jump higher to stay level with her brother. Emitting a sigh of relief, their mother watched for a moment, noticing the rare smile on the face of her son.

"Breakfast will be ready in a few minutes, do you both want scrambled eggs?" Solomon stopped jumping and the smile disappeared from his face. She saw then how frightened he was of her, how many months it had been since she had offered him anything.

"Honey, I'm sorry. I know I was wrong." She opened her arms to take him in. His expression hardened and he looked down, shifting away from her. He still held Mara's hand in his own. Dropping her arms, his mother resumed her apologetic tone.

"I know, sweetie, I know…But we'll have time to make up. I'll make it up to you. I promise. We have time."

"I'm afraid we have no time at all," said the stranger. The children's mother spun to face the voice behind her. The stranger was outlined in the doorway, his huge pack on his shoulders, his hood shading his expression. "I'm afraid that we must leave at once," he finished.

Her reaction was shocked, defensive. "Leave? Where? What do you mean? Why would we leave?" she stammered.

He looked directly into her eyes and answered her carefully, choosing his words. "I'm very sorry. Only the children and I must leave, and leave now. You must stay."

It was as though a heavy weight settled on her, or she somehow deflated. Her body appeared to shrink visibly. Something was very wrong. The children stood uneasily on the bed behind her. She knew this man was not joking, that this was no dream. The nightmare world that she had grown used to was back in her home. She rallied.

"I don't know what the hell you're talking about, mister, but my kids aren't going anywhere with you. Not without me." She spoke with bravado, but her voice betrayed her fear. This gray man was otherworldly and she knew that he was not trying to convince her. He glanced at the frightened children behind her and looked away.

"Perhaps we should speak outside," he said gently.

Sensing his concern for the children, she answered assertively, "Right here is fine and I think we're through talking." She wanted to thank him for what he had done, to make him breakfast and serve him coffee. She wanted the last twelve hours to end in something normal. But he frightened her and telling her that he would take Solomon and Mara was too much for her. She would thank him in her prayers.

"I'm going to have to ask you to leave." She started toward him. She could smell the eggs burning in the kitchen.

"I'm here because of your husband, Thomas. Thomas Worth," he said flatly.

Mara didn't know who Thomas Worth was. She really didn't know that many people at all, other than doctors and nurses, but she saw that her mother and Solomon knew him.

When the stranger said his name, Solomon let go of her hand and his hands balled into tight fists. Her mother took a step backward as if she'd been struck. Many times Mara had seen her mother afraid, afraid for her because she was sick, afraid for Solomon because he was angry, afraid for them all because they were poor, but Mara had never seen her like this. Trembling and faltering, she stopped pretending to be brave.

"Let's talk outside," she said, defeated.

"One moment, please, ma'am," replied the stranger. Removing his pack, he gave her a reassuring look. Squatting and opening it, he extracted two smaller packs, identical to his. He carried them to the bed and deposited both in front of the children. Their mother watched silently, without resisting, as he opened one of the packs, taking out a tightly rolled bundle and a pair of small gray boots. The bundle consisted of a gray hooded tunic similar to the one the stranger wore and a pair of black trousers that were reminiscent of military fatigues. Both were of a rough, textured fabric, and both were sized for a child. The stranger spread them on the bed.

"These are yours, Solomon. Put them on. Look through this pack to see what else you'll need. This pack is also yours, it is very important. It is your life." This last he said with force and authority. He went on, touching the second pack. "This is your sister's. Just like yours. Help her to dress. Your mother and I will be just outside." He walked back toward the door and retrieved his own pack. Gesturing to their mother, he spoke once more to the children. "Pack your packs tightly and neatly. We'll be leaving soon." With that he left the room, the mother following. The door shut and the children were alone.

Outside, on the grass, the stranger began refastening and preparing his own pack. Without taking his eyes from his task, he spoke, "You must have some questions. I can answer at least a few." The mother glared at him bitterly, resentment burning in her eyes.

"Who are you and where are you taking them?"

"The first I can answer, the second I cannot. My true name is not important. I am called Sigil." He finished arranging the straps and flaps on his pack, stood and hefted it to his back.

She spoke again. "Last night I thought you were an angel, sent by God to save her. Now you tell me that *he* sent you. He's been dead for nearly five years. How can an angel work for Thomas Worth?" She spat his name, clenching her fists in frustration.

"No, ma'am. I'm not an angel." He looked at the gray, dirt road running past the house, at the forest beyond it. "I'm something altogether…different." They both heard the kitchen door opening, they paused and looked. The children were dressed. Solomon stepped outside with Mara in tow, he was dressed like the stranger but his trousers were black and his clothes were much less trail-worn. Mara looked the same except her trousers were gray and her black-belted tunic went to just below her knees, giving the appearance of a loose dress worn over pants. Both had small gray backpacks that gave the impression of immensity on such small shoulders and both wore gray leather boots. At the sight of the children, their mother rushed toward them but Sigil held her back with a hand on her shoulder.

"I don't work for your husband and he is not dead," he whispered, his face close to hers. "No harm will come to these children from me and you will see them again. But, you know this must be done, these contracts are not made lightly." She nodded sadly and he let her go. "I'll wait while you say good-bye," he said.

She knelt in front of her children, embracing them each in turn. She had no more tears left to give them. She spoke quickly, seeing the heart-rending confusion on their faces. "Please forgive me, both of you. Forgive me for letting this touch you. I want you both to be brave for me and go with him. His name is Sigil and he knew your father. He will take care of you, I promise." Solomon was looking past her to the figure of Sigil on the road. Mara, not comprehending, hugged her mother.

"Don't worry, Mommy. It's alright, he knows the song that made me better." She liked her new backpack and outfit and she liked Sigil too. "Solomon takes care of me," she stated firmly. Solomon said nothing.

"I love you both so very, very much, and I want you to be careful and come back to me. I want you to promise." She felt the children tugging away from her as Sigil started walking, as if an invisible chain was pulling at them.

"We love you, too," said Mara, "and we promise." Then they were out of her arms, running to catch up with the man in gray, already some distance down the road. She slumped onto her haunches on the grass before the lonely gray house and watched as they fell into step behind him, two steps for every one.

Chapter 9

First Steps

*Of the beginning of the journey
and of their enemies*

THE CHILDREN showed a strength that belied their size and age; Sigil knew the origin of that strength. He periodically glanced back to insure that they were keeping up and, when they were some distance from the gray house, they slipped off of the road and entered the sparse brush that bordered it. The children showed no fear and Mara especially seemed enraptured by the birds and insects that flashed to and fro amidst the trees. Her bright eyes followed the flight of a sparrow between the foliage and bounced along with the butterflies that populated the woods, yet her footsteps were sure and she didn't stumble. Even in the thickest tangle of vines, both children walked like deer, born to the thicket. Sigil led them in this manner for some time, till they were far away from any sign of people. The gray clad man watched the children from the corner of his eye, prepared to offer assistance if they required it but they never did, and he marveled at the ease with which the youngsters negotiated the broken and uneven terrain. It had taken him many years and many miles to move that way in the woods and it was nothing short of magical that both Solomon and Mara were matching him stride for stride. He was also prepared to converse with them if they asked him questions, but Mara was taken by the teeming life around her and Solomon kept to himself, wrapped up inside the fabric of his own hood.

After a time, Sigil broke the silence. "Do either of you wonder why I took you from your home, or perhaps wonder where we are headed?" He slowed slightly so that he could hear their response.

Solomon was the first to speak, "It doesn't matter where we go or why you took us. As long as we don't have to stay there anymore." The boy's face was still hidden inside his hood but the cloth couldn't dull the sharp edge that crept into his small voice. Sigil felt the twinge of pain that the boy gave off and did not fail to notice the same twinge in the face of the girl. He pressed on.

"Do *you* wonder, Mara? Where I am taking you?" he asked. She hopped across a log, her backpack seemingly weightless on her tiny shoulders.

"No," she replied, smiling as she caught sight of a squirrel ducking into a knot in a tree. "I *know* where we're going!" She gleefully trotted on ahead for a few feet, so that she wouldn't lose sight of her new friend. Sigil decided not to pursue the conversation, the little girl mystified him. He had some idea why he had been sent to collect these two children, but they were not yet completely transparent to him. Things were happening around him that were beyond his abilities, he could sense it. He felt tremendous power emitting from Mara and felt a sucking void coming from the boy. He cautiously picked a path through a break in the trees and continued on in silence.

As the daylight began to wane, Sigil began scouting for a suitable place to settle for the night. His concern was for a shelter for the children, for it was about to rain. He looked up between the branches above and saw ominous looking clouds forming in the western sky. He slowed his pace and directed the children to search ahead for kindling on the forest floor as he looked for particular landmarks in the forest. After some time, he spied a cave, cut into a hillside a short distance away. Overtaking the children, he scooped the kindling from their arms and led them to the mouth of the cavern. He peered inside and was about to enter when Mara glided past his legs and into the cave. Nearly dropping the firewood, he gestured to Solomon to follow as he entered the gloomy darkness behind her. Once inside, he called out to her. He didn't need to locate her, he could feel her just beyond his vision. He called out in case she was frightened of the dark, but he felt her heartbeat and realized that he felt more tension in the murky cave than she did. He called out once more and heard her approaching from the throat of the cave. She materialized in the darkness, her wide smile showing in the dusky light that filtered in from the entrance. Sigil dropped the firewood and began to prepare the camp.

Soon there was a small, warm fire burning and as the children watched, the embers cracked and popped away from the logs to float away like fireflies toward the mouth of the cave. The fire cast a low orange sheen over the faces of the traveler and the children and, as the moon rose outside the cave, Sigil began to speak.

"I must tell you both something about the place that I am taking you to, and something about the people that have sent me to collect you." He watched the expressions on their faces and attempted to read their response. Solomon appeared disinterested, almost bored, yet Sigil saw that it was a facade and that the boy was listening closely. Mara's eyes were closing and her small head was leaning toward sleep but when the traveler spoke, she came alive. Alert, she leaned forward to listen to the story. Sigil studied the two young faces that were watching him across the fire and considered his audience. He lightly touched his fingertips together and continued. "There are people who have been interested in both of you since you were born. They have been watching over you and your mother, and they have waited until now to send me for you." He saw that both of the children were awake and listening, so he went on. "These people, they are like you. Not like normal people." The children shifted uncomfortably and Solomon moved to put his arm protectively around his sister's shoulders.

"We *are* normal. What are you talking about?" he replied defensively.

Sigil continued. "You most certainly are not. Of that I am quite sure. You see, I was there when both of you were born. I fought to prevent it from happening." He held up a hand to hold back a startled reaction from the boy. "As you can see, I failed. Before you begin to think that I am the enemy, please, allow me to finish. The people who have sent me, they wish that you be taught. You could think of them as schoolteachers and the place that I am to take you to, well…you could think of it as a school. When you arrive though, you will be the only students in attendance."

"I don't go to school anymore," interjected Mara. "Not since I got sick. Solomon either." She poked at the fire with a stick and watched the end smolder and burst into flame. "I don't even remember my teacher."

"This is a special kind of school, Mara," said Sigil. "It was built just for you and your brother. The teachers have been waiting your whole life to teach you and there's no other place in the world that has teachers like these." He looked out to the horizon that was only partially visible through the portal made by the entrance of the cave. The moon was cut neatly in half as it rose above the rim of the treetops. His voice changed and became lower. "There are some people who don't want you to go to this school at all." As he spoke, he saw Mara's eyes smiling, reflecting in the firelight. She looked toward the entrance too, mimicking his action.

"Like the people outside?" she offered brightly. "The ones in the woods?" He stared at her in disbelief. A look of incredulity spread across his face and he glanced at Solomon to see if Mara was playing a game. Solomon's expression was steady; the child was not playing. Sigil almost could not fathom that the girl had sensed something that he had not, but he recovered quickly and moved silently to the same side of the fire as the children. They reacted to his sudden change of mood instantly and grew uneasy and quiet. He turned to Mara.

"What is it that you hear?" he whispered tersely. "Who is out there?" The girl stared at him wide-eyed, her apprehension being fed by the tone in his voice.

"I can't *hear* them," she whispered back to him. "They have been singing behind us the whole time, in my head. I thought you felt it too." Her forehead wrinkled in consternation. "Am I in trouble? I'm sorry." Sigil waved Solomon behind him and put his hand on Mara's head to reassure her.

"Don't fret, little one, I should have felt that song sooner. It is my fault. Whatever it is that you see me do, just know that it had to be done. Trust me in at least that one thing. They will have seen our fire so we do not have time to waste. Stay behind me until I signal that the path through the entrance is clear." Sigil could now hear the song of their pursuers, a low chant that began as a murmuring sensation in his spine and quickly rose to an irritating drone that was filled with menace. He helped Solomon lift his pack onto his shoulders and gestured to him to help his sister with hers. Then he hefted his own pack and screwed his heels into the gravely floor of the cave. There was no need to extinguish the fire, he knew it was far to late for that so he stood in the orange glow and steadied his breathing.

"There's another way out," whispered Mara. Sigil cast his eyes down at her, his face looked as if it was carved of stone. "That way," she whispered again. He saw in the dim light that her hand was pointing directly to the back of the cave. He did not sense any passage in the cave other than the one they had entered by. He bent slightly.

"Are you certain?" he spoke harshly and did not bother to whisper. The roar of the pursuers song was nearly deafening his thoughts. "Are you certain that it leads out, to the open?" She nodded to him, her face pale and frightened in the dim light. Her brother stood next to her, his hand clasped tightly in hers. Sigil hoped that the boy would not let go. "Run," he said, "I will be behind you." The children stood frozen. "Run!" he repeated, "Solomon, follow her. And no matter what, do not let her go. I will follow you soon." He turned, as the roaring in his head grew total. "RUN!" Behind him, the two children vanished into the darkness.

Four shadowy figures appeared in the entrance to the cave as the children made their escape. Silhouetted in the moonlight, they were cloaked and hooded but Sigil recognized them. Agents of Thomas Worth, beings as much beast as human, they served him as trackers and hunters and assassins.

Sigil grimaced in disgust as they came into view. "Did you actually believe that you would surprise me, with her right beside me?" he spat. The shadows moved silently into the cave as if to encircle the gray clad traveler, but he moved too quickly. He spun in an intricate pattern that intersected the path of the first dark shape and, with a movement that resembled an explosion filmed in reverse and in slow motion, he crouched and pulled himself inward. Then, with blinding speed, as if the film had been suddenly switched to fast-forward, he jammed both fists into the center of the black shroud. The shape grunted and crumpled to the ground at his feet. Sigil continued in a low arc, his boots sweeping through the cinders of the fire, creating a shower of sparks and he finally came to rest in a relaxed position between the other three. One immediately attacked, slashing with such devastating force that the air near Sigil's head was torn with a rending sound. Sigil slid gently to his left and received the energy of the slash with his moving right hand. He guided the strike toward the floor and then slowly and purposefully back toward the face of his attacker. There was a sharp cracking noise that came from within the attacker's cloak. It fell to the floor of the cave atop its accomplice. Sigil turned and faced the remaining pursuers. His breathing was slow and measured as he absorbed the rhythm of their movement. His eyes were nearly closed and he concentrated on the movement of the moon as she rose above the mountain that he was inside of. His enemies were nervous and their fear was disturbing the gentle pull of the moon. Sigil spoke in a soft whisper. "You cannot return to the place from which you came. I cannot allow you to make another attempt for the girl. There is no need to wait. Your fate is inevitable. I'm sorry." The cloaked figures seemed to shudder for a moment and then they struck as one body. There were two smooth yet sudden motions of Sigil's hands and the figures collapsed together. He looked down at the bodies on the floor of the cave and he knelt and made the sign of the cross. His mouth moved in silent prayer and his chin fell to his chest. He completed the prayer and stood. After surveying the scene one final time, he disappeared into the back of the cave.

THE TWO CHILDREN ran hand in hand through the narrow confines of the tunnels that stretched from the back of the cave. Mara led them through the tight and twisting passageways, always sure of where she was. Solomon had no fear that she would lead them astray for he felt that she knew exactly where they were. She had always known where both of them were, and she tugged at his hand with a tension that was both frightened and playful. He could tell that a mixture of fear and a sense of adventure urged her onward. They hurried through the pitch-black tunnels, stepping quickly over stones and crevices as though they had been there many times before. The tunnels became smaller and tighter as they went on and eventually they were crouching and then finally crawling on their hands and knees. Solomon pulled back on Mara's hand anxiously.

"I know that you're not lost, but I'm scared. How much further is it?" He was much stronger than she was, but she pulled against him with such intensity that he nearly lost his grip. "I can't see where your face is Mara, stop for a sec." Mara stopped pulling and he could hear her breathing heavily just below the sound of his own labored breath. "Hold on," he gasped. In the darkness, he felt her trying to sit and he let go of her hand for just a single moment. In a panic, he immediately scrambled to find her hand again. In the short instant that their hands were apart, Solomon felt as though he had lost her in the coal black tunnel and the feeling that she had evaporated into the emptiness that surrounded them was nearly overpowering. He called out to her in terror, but before she could reply he felt her hand in his. He breathed out in relief as his heartbeat began to slow.

"We only have to go a little more," she whispered, her disembodied voice sounding large and hollow inside the caverns. "I think we can get outside up further." She squeezed Solomon's hand and felt it shaking slightly. "Don't worry, I can feel the outside." Solomon knew what she meant but he was unable to feel it. He knew that she didn't mean that she could feel a breeze from an opening or that she could hear noises from the highway. He knew that she meant that she could feel *The World Outside.* He could usually feel it too, but never as clearly as Mara could. He knew that if she felt that feeling that she couldn't be mistaken. It was impossible to mistake that feeling for something else. He relaxed slightly and squeezed back on her hand.

"Ok, let's go. I'm alright now." Their courage replenished, the children started out through the dark tunnel. Solomon cried out first, he saw a small sliver of light ahead of them. "Look!" he exclaimed, "You were right!" He scrambled past her and let go of her hand in his eagerness to reach the light and she flattened against the wall to let him crawl past. The tunnel was bathed in starlight a few feet ahead of them and tiny crystals of ore glistened on the walls of the caves. Solomon rushed forward and caught himself with a sharp intake of breath. They were kneeling at the small mouth of a cave that was cut into the side of an immense wall of stone. Far below them was a carpet of trees laid out in the moonlight. On every side was spread the sky, filled with glowing stars and below, just above the forest, were misty clouds. Solomon pulled himself back away from the edge and reached for Mara's hand. When he did not feel her behind him, he turned to look over his shoulder. What he saw caused him to react in horror. In the muted grays of the moonlight that reflected from the rocks behind her, he saw Mara crawling forward from the cave toward where he sat. Between the two of them curled the huge head of a serpent that was twisting toward Mara as she came into the light. Her eyes were fixed on the ground between her hands as she pulled herself around and past the rough edges of rock. She did not see the venomous hunter as it slid from the crack where it had been slumbering, only to be awakened by Solomon's sharp cry. The boy leapt toward his sister to pull her away from the beast, but the child was too far away. In a dreadful, terrible instant that seemed to go on forever but then it was gone, Solomon saw the snake coil about Mara's waist and pull her over the edge.

Chapter 10

Separation

---

*Of Mara's time in the forest
and of their pursuit*

WITH A FINAL HEAVE, Sigil pulled himself out onto the tiny platform of rock that jutted away from the cliff. He saw the boy seated with his arms wrapped around his knees, a stony look upon his face. Trails of dried tears were etched into a dusty mask that told the traveler the tale of what had happened. He reached into the tunnel behind him and pulled out his pack. Arranging it into a seat, he sat and began to go through one of the many pouches and pockets that were arrayed on it.

The sun was just beginning to cast a rose sheen across the valley far below them when the boy finally spoke. "A snake took her," he said simply. "Before you came." Solomon was dazed and exhausted from panic and weeping and Sigil could see that he was in dire need of rest. Nodding absently at the boy's remark, he continued to tend to his pack. He retrieved a chocolate bar from an outside pocket and offered it good-naturedly to Solomon but the boy seemed to look completely through it. Sigil took a bite and chewed thoughtfully as he watched the sun rise over the distant forest. Solomon stared at the ground in front of him and went on. "It was so fast. I couldn't see where she went. I tried to climb down but I couldn't see..." He faltered, his voice trailing off into sobs. "She fell over the edge!" he finally choked out. Sigil finished the chocolate and wiped his hands on his trousers, and then he brought his hands to his shoulders and partially raised his hood. The morning mist was cold and brittle in that high and lonely place. He considered his words carefully.

"When the snake took her, what did it look like?" he asked gently, careful to avoid the boy's vacant stare. "Describe it to me."

"It was horrible...it just wrapped around her before I saw it there. Before I could stop it." He looked at the section of the edge where he had seen his sister last, as if she might somehow reappear there.

"No, I mean, what did the snake *look* like?" returned Sigil. "Was it big? Small? What color was it? How did it act? Describe to me what you saw." Solomon seemed like he was about to react angrily to the questions but then he sighed and seemed to shrink with weariness.

"It was so dark, I don't know what color it was. It was a huge snake, like this…" He held up his hands to show Sigil. "I think it was a python," he continued, "I saw one at the museum one time and it looked like that. It was evil." His voice wound down as he dropped his head. Sigil focused on the last words that he had said.

"Why do you say that it was evil?" he asked. "What makes you say that?" The boy looked up at him.

"It took her away! They fell down there!" He pointed at the edge and looked at Sigil as if he were mad, as if the hooded man did not understand what he had said. Solomon was angry now. "Don't you even care?" He scowled at Sigil with real hatred.

"Answer my question, boy!" snapped the traveler. His voice wrapped around Solomon the way it had when they had first met, calming the child and reassuring him. This time it was different though, Sigil's tone was urgent, in a way that he had not shown before. He had not wished to frighten the boy.

Solomon answered him. "It was evil, I could tell," he said sullenly. Sigil was not appeased.

"How?" he pressed.

Solomon examined his memory of the chaotic events of the night before. "It looked at her, before it took her," he whispered, almost to himself. "I saw how it looked at her, like it had seen her before." He could only now, in the light of the rising sun, remember the face of the serpent and the memory of it set his skin crawling. He shivered.

"Put your hood up, boy!" laughed Sigil, "I have seen that snake before!" Solomon stared at him incredulously, baffled by his sudden change of mood. "Your sister has survived the fall, I am certain of it. I only had to be sure that we had crossed paths with *that* particular snake. He may think that she is just a little girl, but from what I have been told about the two of you, she will prove to be more than a match for him. Calm your heart, Solomon, and get some rest. Mara is alive, rest assured. Sleep now, and when you wake, I'll finish the story that was interrupted late last night. When you hear it, you will finally understand. And then, we will find Mara."

TEMPTING AND MALICIOUS, the serpent cast a baleful gaze upon the terrified child. Shivering and mute with fright, the small girl held her eyes tightly shut and curled into a ball at the foot of the mountain. The last thing that she remembered was falling slowly, as if she had been dreaming her way down the side of the cliff. The snake stiffened and extended its neck, then brought its cold tongue within inches of her cheek and began to methodically fold coils of scaly muscle around her throat. Deep within the paralysis that gripped her, she felt a rumbling, a tremor that began in her belly and made her feel full and swollen and aching. She struggled against the tightening grip of the reptile but could not move, the monster's strength was far greater than her own. The rumbling inside of her grew in intensity and permeated into the serpent, which responded by increasing the pressure on her fragile windpipe. She gasped and choked and started to sob softly, yet she did not panic and the tremor grew into a violent jerking that threatened to smash both her and the snake into pieces against the granite face of the rock. A soft glowing luminescence began to exude from the child's head and a raw, primal heat reflected from the serpent's eyes. The child was aflame with energy and it leached into the slope behind her. At first, small stones began to crack and crumble away from the face of the mountain. Then, and with a steadily increasing fury, greater and greater stones separated and shaled away from the cliff. The snake felt it, a change in the balance of power between them, an empty void where the snake's primitive strength had been. In fear and confusion, the serpent attempted to unravel its coils from the little girl's neck but it was too late, the bargain was sealed. The monster had taken something from the child and the payment was to be immediate, its scaled skin was already charring in places and a rancid, burning odor was filling the air. In a few moments it was over. The snake was dead and burning and Mara stood and looked down at the smoking worm at her feet. She did not know that what had just happened to her was unusual at all. She shook the straps of her backpack into a more comfortable position and started down the trail that she found at the foot of the mountain.

SOLOMON OPENED HIS EYES and saw the pink hue of the fading sunlight. He slowly looked around through the remaining vestiges of sleep. He'd had nightmares while he slept and Sigil had stayed close to him, only moving off once during the day to search for a likely route down. As consciousness returned, he suddenly realized how long he had slept. He sat sharply upward, searching quickly about for his pack.

"Come on, we have to go!" he erupted, "We have to find my sister!" Sigil motioned for him to remain still.

"I told you. I have a story to finish. Mara is safe for now. You of all people should know that. Haven't you ever wondered why you can always tell if she is safe or in danger? If she is healthy or ill?" He handed Solomon the pack that he had been groping for and gestured that he should sit. "You need to understand some things about where we are going, and how it came to be that your four year old sister could fall six-hundred feet in the dead of night and laugh as though it is a game that she is playing. Come now, Solomon, do you mean to tell me that you have never thought about the strange or unusual *differences* that you and Mara possess? Have a seat and hear my tale. You just may find it to be a story that you already know." Solomon slowly sat back on his pack and looked guilty, as if Sigil had caught Mara and him in a game that they were forbidden to play. He felt as if a closely guarded secret, something private and special that he and his sister had shared, was exposed. He felt naked and vulnerable. No one, not even his mother, had ever been aware of the link between the two of them, and now this stranger, who had only just met them yesterday, already knew. He knew so much that it worried Solomon; he wanted to keep people out of the space that he and Mara shared. It was the only place where he felt safe. The only place where he felt powerful. He eyed the traveler warily and remained silent, pretending that none of it bothered him, but to Sigil, he was transparent.

The gray hooded stranger had the mercy to look away from the bitter little boy as he settled on his pack and began speaking. "What has your mother taught you about Heaven and Hell?" he asked.

MARA WAS DEEP in the forest that skirted the tall mountain from which she had fallen, and was walking ever deeper. She had realized right away that the way to go was not back up the mountain, and so she started to explore and play in the silence and enormity that was the woods. She saw crowds of colorful birds scatter at her arrival, and it delighted her when they allowed her to get closer each time. She watched a family of deer as they fed in a clearing, the antlers of the father buck rising majestically as he heard her approach. She knew that the fawn was her friend and that the father was simply doing his duty, protecting his child. She stepped on the slippery rocks that made a bridge across a stream that was just her size and she felt that she had found the finest playground in the world. The serpent from earlier had been forgotten, like part of a movie that she was not allowed to watch because it was too scary. She had sometimes sneaked to the crack in her door and seen parts of those movies, but she had never been frightened. She knew that none of it could hurt her. The only thing that had ever hurt her was the thing that had made her so sick, and nothing like that was in these woods. She felt that Solomon was upset and sad and she thought of trying to get back to where she had been but she wanted him to come to her. These woods were so much better than the dark caves and the tall mountain. He would come to get her; he would never forget where she was. Until he came to pick her up, she would keep herself busy like when she used to play by herself when she couldn't leave her bed. When she thought about how she used to play, it reminded her of her bear, Brownie, and she stopped next to a fallen log to remove her backpack. For a brief moment she spun round in circles as she struggled to get the pack off; it was the first time she had to do it by herself so it was hard, but she quickly sorted it out. She sat on the log, opened the top flap of her pack and rummaged through it until she produced her tattered, brown teddy bear.

"There you are, Brownie," she addressed him. "It must be stuffy in there! I promise that I won't leave you in there anymore unless I have to." She stretched and pulled the bear's arms and legs in an attempt to smooth his fur, then she clung tightly to the stuffed animal as she put on her backpack, switching him from hand to hand so that he wouldn't get dirty. When she had everything in place once again, she and her companion resumed their exploration.

ON THE LEDGE high above the carpet of trees, Sigil was relating to Solomon the story of his young life.

"For many years, the people of this world have had a belief in Heaven and Hell. In all cultures, in all countries, there is an abiding feeling that the universe is split into two factions. Do you know what a faction is, Solomon?" Solomon shook his head. "It means team, or maybe a side that you can be on, you follow?" The boy nodded, looking slightly confused. "Just follow along, you will see clearly soon enough. In your country and your culture, most people think of these things as a story, or a myth. They think of them as symbols for ideas. They don't think of them as real, like you or me, or like this rock here." He picked up a stone to illustrate his point. "They are mistaken. For as long as history has been written, and even for many centuries before that, there has been a small group of men and women on this planet that know that these things are true. Not believe it. *Know* it." He paused, checking to see that the boy was paying attention. "In olden times, there were fairy tales, like the ones that they tell children these days. Do you know any fairy tales?" He stopped and waited for Solomon's answer.

"Sure," the boy replied, "Hansel and Gretel, Snow White. I know what you mean."

"Think about what you just said," returned Sigil, "Why are those stories called fairy tales? There are no fairies in them. As a matter of fact, the only things in those stories that are not 'real' are..." He waited, prompting Solomon.

"Umm...the witches, I guess," finished Solomon.

"Good guess, the witches. When we think of the tales and legends and even the religious stories, there is a common thread that runs through them. We think of the supernatural. I know that you know what that means. People, or beings that seem like people, who can do things that normal people cannot. Super people. Supernatural. Think about some stories from the Bible that you know. Did your mother ever take you to church?"

"No, not that I remember. I know some of the stories though."

Sigil stopped him. "Which stories do you remember?" he asked. "Do you know where your name comes from, why your father named you so?" He watched Solomon's face closely for any telltale sign or reaction to the questions that he was asking.

"He named me after a king," said Solomon. "A famous king."

"All of the kings in the Bible are famous. But you are correct, that particular king is one of the most famous. He was famous for a few things, he was famous because he could speak to animals, and he was very wise. He was famous because he rebuilt a very important temple in a very important city. And he was famous because he was very skilled at magic." Sigil paused so that the boy could speak.

"What kind of magic?" Solomon asked. His curiosity had arisen, in spite of his impatience.

Sigil thought for a moment. Then, as though he had come to the answer reluctantly and had been compelled to say it, he replied, "The only kind there is."

MARA HEARD the low boom of thunder as it rolled through the green spaces beneath the tree branches. The sky was darkening rapidly and the hot summer breeze blew harder than before. She had never been outside in a rainstorm and when the first large drops splashed off of the leaves just above her, she looked up to see great, gray clouds between the limbs of the trees. She felt electricity in the air and could smell the power of the storm as it picked up its primal energy. She was excited, but she was worried about Brownie. He had only been in the washing machine at home and he had hated it, so she had to stop again to put him away.

"Sorry, but you'll have to get wrinkled again. I don't want you getting all wet and messing up all the rest of our stuff." She had no sooner finished packing him neatly away, than she found herself in the center of a torrential summer storm. The rain came in thick bursts and soon gray veils hid the woods. The wind tore at the wayward child and buffeted her from one side of the path to the other. She heard the low continuous roar of the torrent and heard within it a throbbing hum, growing stronger and more pronounced as she struggled against the strength of the storm. It seemed as if the storm itself was astonished at the perseverance of the tiny wanderer. With juvenile temerity, Mara pushed through the gale and closed on the sound that she heard beneath the wind.

Chapter 11

History

*Of the origin of the children
and of the task that they face*

SOLOMON was listening to Sigil speak with rapt attention. The mention of magic caused him to lean toward the traveler, his eyes wide.

"You see, Solomon, people like your father and others, people like... well, myself. We know, we *remember* that magic isn't a thing to be studied or learned. It cannot be taught. It isn't what your world has been made to believe. Magic isn't even something to believe, or to believe in. It simply *is*. Like electricity or magnetism. Both of those forces existed even when there was no circuit or magnet to harness them. They were there before the animal man devised tools to manipulate them. In point of fact, the devices that you see in this era, the ones that rely on electrical impulses and circuitry, they are an outgrowth of the original, primal magical urge."

Sigil looked to see if Solomon understood. When he saw that he did, he went on. "All of those creatures, the ones that you've heard of in the stories, the ones that you've read about and seen on television, they come from the same place. Many years ago, long before men walked the earth, before the history of man even speculates, there were battles here. Great battles that were the final struggles of an even greater war. Creatures of pure light, creatures that are unlike the people that we see today, they waged war here. And they were, in the end, finally left here. Call it banishment, or imprisonment, or abandonment. You could even say that they fled to this refuge. However you choose to describe it, these beings are your ancestors. In essence, they are the ancestors of all of the beings on this planet that are endowed with souls, but you and your sister are their direct descendants. There was an order created, a group of men and women who dedicated their lives to remaining in contact with those of original, untainted stock. But they were... tempted. Impatient. They were unable or unwilling to wait until God decided that it was time for the exiled to return home and they thought that they had found a loophole, a way around waiting. Mara is that loophole."

Solomon looked thoughtfully at the clouds that filled the sky above and below them. His expression was wistful. "We came from the stars…" He spoke in reverie, with a sense of nostalgia that seemed out of place in someone so young. "I used to dream about being in space when I was little. The dreams seemed so *real*, not like a regular dream but like I could remember it. Like I had really been there. There were lights, and colors that weren't like the colors here. And there was music." His voice faded as he looked deeply into the gathering clouds. "And there were lots of us. I wasn't alone."

Sigil nodded and answered him, "I remember it as well. And no, you weren't alone. You only cannot remember it as anything more than a dream. Most cannot remember at all. I was there with the others but the others never rebelled. They are what you would call Angels. Beings that come from the heavens, beings made of light, of pure energy. They are not as they are portrayed in your modern culture. They are the warriors of a long forgotten war. The ones that managed to survive the rebellion came here to lick their wounds and to regroup and to wait for any opportunity to return to their home. Some decided to stay and they mixed with the creatures that had been placed here by The Most High. This is where the stories of elves and fairies, fauns and centaurs came from. This regression enraged the powers of heaven. Almost every person walking on this planet is the offspring of those times. You and Mara are not. You were created so that your father would have a direct link to the source."

Solomon reacted to Sigil's mention of his father. He snapped his head quickly toward the older man, a look of dismay and anger on his face. "What do you mean, we were *created*?" he questioned. "I don't understand."

Sigil took a breath before he went on and approached the subject gingerly. "Your father participated in a ritual and signed a contract so that he would be allowed to return. The price that was to be paid was Mara. If she were to die here in the flesh as a sacrifice, then your father would be able to regain his station. He would become a being of light again. I was sent to stop that sacrifice. I have business of my own with your father. But now the Order is split, divided. Some believe that you should take your father's place here and that your sister should die, that she would become far too powerful if she lived. In their eyes, she was born only to die, to be sacrificed and she was never supposed to walk this earth. If she had been sacrificed, you would have succeeded your father as the leader of the Order here on Earth, and he would have risen. Your sister is something far from human; she is the crystallization of light in human form. She was only supposed to be alive long enough for your father to pay his debt and for the earthly, temporal power to pass into you, but with our help, your mother was able to escape with you and your newborn sister and remain undiscovered. We waited as long as possible before acting, but your sister would not have survived without our intervention for much longer. From a distance, through both space and time, your father was slowly poisoning her."

The two of them sat on the ledge in silence for a while. Solomon played with the stones that were gathered between his boots and thought about the images he had of his father. There were very few, just scattered memories that were mostly bits and pieces of stories that his mother had told them. He thought of somebody hurting Mara and his fists clenched. He squeezed the gravel in his hand until it cut.

"What are we supposed to do then?" he asked, seeing the smear of blood on the stones that he held.

"Magic, as you know it from the legends, is fading," said Sigil. "It has been since the Fall from Heaven. Men were once powerful and nearly immortal, but now man has only a very weak link with the ethereal. As time passed and generations descended from higher to lower on this plane, technology began to replace mysticism as the technique to manipulate energy. Our race, led by your father, has engaged in a systematic acquisition of all the energies on the planet. There is a drought of spiritual energy; your father and his followers have monopolized the last remaining non-tech sources left. Our magic is weak but not entirely destroyed. Your sister is the key right now, at this particular point in space and time."

"We have to find her," said Solomon. "Before my father does."

Sigil nodded his agreement. "We will. We are not alone in this wilderness and your sister is not without her own defenses." He smiled inwardly.

"There is still more that I should tell you," he continued. "There was a prophecy and a curse. I was the cause of it. Because of my disobedience, I was placed on this battlefield. There will be another war. It will begin very soon and when it is finished, there will be no magic remaining here. There will be only technology. Hell itself will have descended on this place. Or this place will have descended into Hell. This is preordained and cannot be altered, but the prophecy claims that there will be one creature of God left among these half-breeds. There will be a solitary, descended human who still remains who can sing the Litany. Mara is not the descended one, but she may be the only one that can protect the descended one from your father."

"How can she protect anyone?" asked Solomon angrily. "She's only a little kid. *I'm* only a little kid! Why should we have to go to school to learn this stuff? We weren't the ones who started all of this."

The interruption caused Sigil to glance sharply at him. "All of these things are connected, Solomon. You and your sister were there when this began. You were only in another form, as was I. You are simply unable to remember this. That is a blessing from The Most High, one that I have had taken away from me. Passage through time and space is a power and a curse that I am forced to carry, I carry the curse of memory. I see the changes that our whole race endures, and I remember the song that we once sung. We are all responsible, you no less than I, and we have no time to throw away on attempts to hide from that fact."

Solomon thought about what Sigil said and knew that it was true, somehow he felt that the story the gray hooded traveler told was familiar, as though he could tell it just as well. Only if he told it, he would feel as though he was making it all up.

The traveler broke into the boy's thoughts, "This war will not be like other wars before it," he said. "Throughout the history of this world, magic has been declining. This war will be fought over the last strongholds of it, using the last remnants of it. The Order itself only realizes the smallest amounts of the magical powers that remain untapped. True magic relies on creative intellect, the ability to hold an image in ones mind and to create it here on Earth. The cathedral builders and composers, the sculptors and painters, they are the vestigial extensions of the original Angelic force. They are actually exercising the same powers that were used in celestial combat during the original rebellion. The Order is aware of this. The enemy will not attack military targets, they will attack museums, or libraries, or universities, do you understand? The human spirit itself will be under siege. It will be up to us to stage a counter to this erosion of the mind. This will be the final act in the drama that The Most High has arranged for this world." He stood and beckoned to Solomon to do the same. "And do not overlook the fact, Solomon, that you were warned not to let go of your sister's hand." Solomon's face flushed red with humiliation and sorrow. Sigil knew that it was cruel to remind the boy of his mistake, but he also knew that greater cruelties than that were possible if he were ever to make another.

Searching through his pack, Sigil produced two lengths of rope, one very short, and another much longer one. He motioned to Solomon to find a short rope of his own inside his pack. He showed the boy how to tie the rope into an improvised climbing harness and how to check and tighten the knots. He then showed him how to find the mid-point of the longer rope and to loop it around a strong outcropping of rock with the two trailing ends lying ready by the edge. He explained that they would then be able to retrieve their rope when they were at the bottom and he explained the how and why of keeping the rope untangled. When they were ready, he instructed Solomon in the techniques of rappelling down the jagged face of the mountain and tossed the ends of the rope over the edge.

"Here is where you would shout 'Rope!', Solomon," said Sigil in a low voice. "But with the enemy in pursuit of us, we will leave that for another time. Are you ready?" He saw the fear on Solomon's face and made an effort to reassure him. "I will be on the ledge just below you, you won't be able to slide past me. Just remember to brake the way that I taught you and you will not fall. Keep your brake hand extended to your side and brake by putting your hand in the small of your back. Have courage, we must do this before we can find Mara." Solomon swallowed and seemed frozen on the rope, he looked fearfully over his shoulder at the gray hooded man behind him. "I will be right below you," repeated Sigil and then he slipped over the edge. Solomon gripped the rope in his right hand tightly, he was afraid to look over the edge. He felt the tension give way on the rope and heard Sigil's voice rise softly from below him. "I have you on belay. Come, just like I taught you." He anxiously slid his heels back across the gravel, a single inch at a time, slowly creeping toward the edge. When his boots were hanging halfway in empty space, he leaned backwards into nothingness and looked behind and below him. His breath caught sharply in his throat, Sigil was nowhere to be seen. There was nothing but the sheer wall of the cliff face, curving away from his vision and, far beyond it, the forest floor. He saw the curling mist of cloud below him and saw hawks wheeling in the updrafts of wind. He froze once again, unable to release his grip on the rope that was jammed into the small of his back. The weight of his backpack pulled against the front of his shoulders and he felt the rope stretch. His chest felt tight and he felt unable to breathe. He was thinking fervently of trying to pull his way back into a vertical position when the rope suddenly slid an inch.

"Sigil!" he gasped, "I ... can't!" He felt the rope burning into his left hand, extended in front of him. In a panic, he started to lean forward. The forest spun below him.

"Lean back!" said Sigil forcefully. "I'm right here, lean back onto your heels as I showed you." Solomon leaned backwards and the forest floor righted itself once again. "Walk back towards my voice on your heels, I am just below." Solomon obeyed and began descending the cliff. In a few moments he was standing on a ledge next to Sigil. "Very well done, I've seen many do much worse than you on their first try. I've seen those who could not even do it at all, so do not lose heart." Solomon reddened at the praise but he felt much better. "We have a few more bounds to go. Do you feel up to it?" The boy nodded determinedly. They exchanged places on the rope and continued down the cliff.

MARA FOLLOWED THE NOISE as it throbbed and hummed just beyond her sight. She knew that it was always ahead of her and that it was moving. It brought to her mind the game of hide and seek and she was good at hide and seek because she was patient. Patience was a trait that an invalid child could develop in great strength; to be bed-ridden for most of her life had created fortitude in Mara that was far beyond that of a normal child. The rain began to fade to a drizzle and the hum became louder and more pronounced, yet it stayed just out of the reach of Mara's vision. She felt that it was playing with her, she could sense that its mood was playful, and in the keener vision of her mind's eye, she could also tell that it was female, and a child, like her. As the last of the rain drifted away, the sun began to shine misty streaks through the tented ceiling of leaves and Mara stopped to extract Brownie from his confinement. As she pulled the bear into the first rays of sunlight, she caught a reflected glimpse of the child that she had been playing with. Floating in the path before her was a glowing being with wings like a dragonfly's. Shaped like a tiny, perfectly formed doll, it had fiery hair and eyes like electric sparks.

The creature saw that she was discovered and came close to Mara, causing her eyes to widen in amazement, and offered a greeting, "Welcome, Mara..." The corners of Mara's eyes crinkled in delight and wonder, as she reached up to touch the fairy, for that was what it was. The fairy stretched out a delicate arm and daintily shook Mara's proffered hand. "Mara, this is Father Dante," she said, "Father Dante, Mara Worth."

Standing before her in a small clearing in the woods was a gray-bearded man wrapped in a brown, woolen monk's habit. Other, more youthful men in similar garb surrounded him on all sides. The top of the man's head was shaved bald and he had kind, glittering eyes which he aimed at the little girl that stood at the limit of the trees. She had never

seen anyone who looked remotely like him or his compan-
ions and she smiled as she saw the shining spot atop his
head, bordered by wisps of gray hair. She thought he looked
wildly funny and she spread her smile wider. Her shyness
overcame her though and she looked back toward the forest
floor, but she continued to smile at the leaves that swirled in
gusts around her boots.

Dante had looked up and seen Mara standing before
him. His weathered face had cracked into a smile that
seemed like a long forgotten memory that had suddenly returned from the corners of his mind. She looked up at him in
wonder, mesmerized by the light that surrounded him and
the others that were standing in the wood by his side. She
held her stuffed bear like a shield in front of her and shyly
smiled in return. She turned her face away, blushing.

"Where is your guardian, little one? The tall man in
gray? How is it that you appear to us in these woods without your guide?" Mara didn't reply, she knotted her fingers into Brownie's fur and lifted her eyelids up to see if
Dante was watching her. He was, and so she quickly returned her eyes to her hands, busily arranging the coat of
her bear. Tiny beings with glowing wings flitted to and fro
through the clearing and they seemed familiar to Mara, she
knew them all, as though they were classmates from her last
school. They seemed distracted, torn between greeting her
and performing some task that she could not see.

"Fear not, your brother and Sigil shall be here soon. I
sense them on your trail even now. I'm sure that they had
quite a scare, losing you like that, but *you* never lost *them*
did you, child?" He patted her head as she shook it proudly;
Dante went on, "No, I'm sure that you had your mind's eye
on them the entire time that you were playing, didn't you?"
Mara nodded, beaming. "That was very lucky for them that
you were guarding them! Ahhh, here are the culprits now."

She spun to see Solomon and Sigil trotting up the path that she had walked on. Her face shone with a smile as she ran to her brother and embraced him.

He returned the embrace with relief and squeezed her tightly. "I'm so sorry Mara, I tried to stop you from falling. I swear I did." Tears welled in Solomon's eyes as he re-lived the scene of his sister sliding over the edge of the cliff, held firmly in the coils of the serpent. "Please believe me. Please?" He looked imploringly at her, seeking forgiveness in her round smiling face. Her joy at being reunited with her brother outshone any fear he might have of her being angry with him. He saw in her innocence and trust.

"I'm okay!" she laughed. "Are you okay? I'm sorry I fell. I won't let go of your hand again. Okay?" She reached out and put Solomon's hand in her right hand and Sigil's hand in her left. Together they followed Father Dante and the others on a winding path between the trees.

The Third Tale

The Order of Dismas

Chapter 12

The Contract

*Of the bargain of Thomas Worth
and of the payment promised*

Nine years earlier - Tibet

HE had disciplined himself and mortified his flesh. He had sacrificed years of earthly pleasure and temporal comfort. It was to culminate in this. This ritual was the key to his rebirth into the celestial hierarchy, his destined return to his rightful place at the head of his legion. Thomas Worth was far ahead of the guides that had escorted him to this final ascent. He was alone on the mountain. He looked up and ahead and saw the unblemished snow that blanketed the glacier. High above it, he saw the monastery, a mass of tightly mortised stone, rising like a steeple, capping the top of the slope. He trudged onward, his poles biting through a thick crust of ice and tearing into the snow beneath it. Sweat soaked the inner layer of his parka and trousers and his breath came in shallow, panting surges. He was in excellent physical condition, but this final assault on the mountain was enough to try the strength of even the most accomplished mountaineer. A grim determination dragged him upward.

It was nightfall before he arrived at the entrance to the monastery. He waited, sitting with his back to the giant ornate portal that served as a gate, regaining his strength and mentally preparing himself. He gazed absently across the long length of stairs that he had ascended, each step carved by hand centuries ago, cut out of the mountain by long dead monks. Before long, the gate opened and he was waved inside. He had been expected.

The lama, an ancient, stooped figure, wrapped in a cowl of matted furs, greeted Thomas silently, flanked on both sides by other monks. Without speaking, Thomas followed the lama and his retinue as they led him through the monastery halls and into a cavernous prayer room. The lama gestured to two of the young novices and they noiselessly drifted into the shadows that edged the chamber, only to return with candles grasped in their hands. There were more monks along the periphery of Thomas' vision, holding drums and bamboo flutes and the gentle dirge that they played cast a pall over the darkened room. The floor was covered with a giant mandala, etched permanently into the stone and dyed a myriad of colors, the geometry radiating away from the center and fading into black as the light from the candles failed and died away. Thomas walked to the center of the mandala and lowered himself into a lotus position, his legs tied into the knot pattern, his spine settling and aligning above it. He rested the back of his right hand onto his right knee and gently touched the tip of his thumb to his middle finger. His left hand was held aloft, his palm facing forward, his fingers curled softly into an arcane salute. His eyes were rolled back into his head, their lids held halfway open and flickering slightly. He began his mantra.

There was a murmur that resonated throughout the prayer room and Thomas focused it into his center. He pulled the chanting of the monks into his body and felt it vibrate down and then back up his spine. Rocking gently in time with the chanting, he saw a light grow in his mind's eye: at first, a small, dim spark, growing finally into an intense burn. His eyes were fully closed and in the darkness of his own mind, from within the light in the center, he saw a shape begin to form. The shape was geometric and symmetrical; it did not seem organic or natural. Nor did it seem like the hand of man had made it. It was as though a three-dimensional shape had a greater number of sides to it than could be represented in normal thought. It was formed of more than four dimensions, it was a polytope. The shape grew from the thoughts of Thomas and formed in the air above him. The lama, seated and facing Thomas from across the mandala, folded his hands and closed his eyes as well. Above him a similar shape manifested.

To a being that is immortal, the notion of time holds no sway. Along with time, space is also done away with. Thomas was not mortal like the monks that surrounded the mandala. True enough, his body would fade and rot away as would every other body in the temple, but he was aware of the nature of how his soul would be translated, and so this caused his soul to live on in a continued state, life after life. This awareness had been won at a dear price; he had sacrificed much in order to realize it. He was one of the few men on earth who did. The aged lama who watched him from across the temple floor also knew his own, true nature and, like the other souls who had become aware, he remembered Thomas from before the Fall.

The lama adjusted his hands, knotting his wizened fingers into a posture of supplication, and allowed the tone that emitted from his throat to change pitch and timbre. Thomas saw that the lama waited for him to initiate the ritual. He saw the polytope in his mind's eye and stretched his imagination until it touched his will. When the two were combined, he formed the structure of an idea. No sooner had the idea entered his mind than the combined sound of the gathered monk's voices changed and grew in volume. Thomas began to alter the sound of the drone that came from the monks. It modulated and shifted in response to his will, rising and falling according to his whim, as though he played on a musical instrument, the rooms and hallways of the monastery itself forming the pipes of a huge stone flute. The drone of the chant began to shape itself first into a melody and then, it separated into harmony. As the music emerged, the shapes that floated in the air above them solidified.

"What fools dare to disturb our slumber?" The voice that spoke from the center of the hovering shape was grotesque. It formed itself out of the discordant throb of the humming that rose from the throats of the monks and it grated and clashed with itself. An equally disturbing voice came from the shape above the lama.

"Yesss," it hissed, "Who are the creatures resssponsible?" The two shapes were now quite solid, yet neither Thomas nor the lama opened their eyes or acknowledged that they saw the beings.

Thomas spoke in a whisper. "I am the one who calls on you both. I do so of my own free will, as has been granted me by The Most High and has been our privilege since the agreement and the treaty. I do so with full and willing knowledge of the price and I do so with no enmity. We have been allies before this time and I now invoke thee with thy true and given names." He croaked a guttural sound that cut through the din of the chanting monks and the shapes glowed brightly, then faded quickly.

"Ahhh, it is you, Lord Berith…We recognize you now. It can be difficult to see through the armor of flesh that you wear. We are at your service." Both shapes bowed in deference to the seated form of Thomas. "What is it that you require?" Thomas did not move or respond in any physical way. He simply spoke through the chanting with his mind.

"I wish to strike a bargain," he began, "I wish to regain my rightful place. I wish all that and more." He opened his eyes and fixed them on the shape that drifted in the smoke above the lama and his eyes burned into it. The being that looked back at him saw the rage and fury that he barely held in check. Thomas saw the monk that sat across from him and surveyed the company of monks that surrounded him. There had been years of pain and preparation that had gone into this moment and he was nearly unable to retain his composure. Through gritted teeth and slitted eyes, he spoke again, "I will gladly pay the price that is required."

THOMAS HAD MENTIONED a bargain and he had also mentioned that there would be a price to pay. The price was to be agreed upon before the ritual could go any further. The two spirits that hovered above the company that was gathered in the prayer room did not negotiate on their own behalf; rather they spoke as proxies for unwritten laws and long forgotten pacts. They were messengers for beings that were much more powerful than they were, for that was what the word angel meant: 'messenger'. Thomas was aware that the price, whatever it happened to be, would be beyond his understanding. Since he had become imprisoned in the flesh and forced to live through countless deaths and rebirths, he had become clouded and distracted. There had been many times that he had completely forgotten his rank and station; he had forgotten that he had once been a commander in the company of Heaven. During those times he had lived like an animal, eating and drinking, fornicating and fighting, exactly like the animals that they had come to the Earth to corrupt. He had forgotten that he had once been a duke in the company of Hell, a leader of the legions that had led the rebellion in the stars. He had only the vaguest of recollections of the sights and sounds that he had once experienced and when he had, they had come to him as dreams and wisps of memories, or drunken hallucinations or when he was deep in meditation. It had taken him generations to put the memories together into a coherent whole. Lifetime after lifetime, studying and researching, leaving clues for himself to find in the next life and finally coming to self-realization. When he had, the memories came to him in flashing gushes, nearly driving him mad with ecstasy and shame, but he had prevailed and through that prevalence, he had arrived here at this monastery. He had arranged the ritual and had paid these dark monks their blood money. Now, he was about to receive the ceremony that would restore him to his original immortal state. He had full knowledge that whatever the price was, it would make no coherent sense to a mortal man. He remembered what it had been like to peer into the vast reaches of space and time, to think in infinite dimensions and to contemplate creation itself. He had prepared himself and had vowed to show fortitude that befitted a celestial, not a mortal, and he prepared himself now as he sat in the lotus beneath the hovering spirits.

"What shall the price be for the ritual, and how shall it be paid?" he intoned.

The spirit that sat in the air above the lama spoke for both. "The price shall be trivial," spoke the spirit, "and there shall be no deviation from our commands. You have subordinate entities on this mortal plane?"

"Of course," answered Thomas. He had devoted years to pulling himself up the ladder of the world's occult orders. He had spent this lifetime and the one before it, and the one before that. He had mortals who would die for him and quite a few who lived for him. There were always those who would trade what little blessings they had for the chance to gain more. "What shall I do to satiate you and your masters?"

The being burned brightly as it responded. "You shall mate with a virgin mortal," it began, "and you shall invoke the *****." Here, the spirit spoke an unintelligible syllable that could not be repeated by a human tongue. Thomas heard it and he shivered with a shock of recognition. The spirit went on, "She shall bear two children, a male child and a female. The male shall carry the weight of the Anchor. He shall be the ballast that will take away your humanity. To create such a being, the female child shall be cleansed of the stain of sin from her birth. She shall pour her wickedness into the boy and he shall carry her weight. This female must not live in the flesh, Lord Berith. Do you understand?" Thomas nodded as the thoughts of how he would arrange such circumstances began to form in his mind. He heard the spirit's disembodied voice continue outside of his plotting. "She must be sacrificed to pay the price that has been levied on the boy. She must be sacrificed in the name of our masters. Are you willing to pay this price, Lord Berith? Can you pay while wearing this mortal flesh, Thomas Worth?"

The seated man lifted his head to the spirits above him and nodded forcefully and spoke in reply. "I gladly accept the bargain and duly promise to pay the price. I shall spawn the half-breed child and pour his purity into his celestial sister. I understand the toll that must be paid and understand the levy."

The spirit spoke again, "But do you understand the risk, Thomas Worth?" he asked, using Berith's mortal name. "If the girl is not sacrificed to us, then *you* shall be the sacrifice. If she walks the Earth, then you shall be the toll that we collect."

Thomas Worth raised his head and spoke in a low voice, "She will be created by my will, and she will die by my hand."

Chapter 13

The Abbey

The Order

Fade like the mist of the summer's dawn
Never be held even when seen
Strike with the shock of the Thunder's bolt
Delivered unyielding to those who have been
Chosen through acts or through words or misdeeds
As worthy opponents of this black souled clan
Thieves in the night, yea plotters, assassins
We drink like fine wine the fears of a man
We walk through walls.
Untouchable...

THE CHILDREN were taken to the place where they were to receive instruction. The Abbey was a white stone chapel, hidden in the center of a large city. It sat quietly behind ivy covered granite block walls, surrounded on all sides by taller, more conventional buildings, and from outside its small courtyard only the steeple could be seen. An imposing, black iron gate guarded the entrance.

Before they arrived, Father Dante related to them the story of the Abbey, as he knew it. The legend of the chapel was that once, long ago, it had sat in the center of a great forest that had grown in that same spot. The chapel had been dedicated to the memory of the daughter of the builder of the structure, a man who had lost his child to the wickedness of the world. The daughter was to have become a nun, a bride of Christ, but she had been tempted, and so she had become a daughter of The World. For many generations, Father Dante's order had maintained the chapel, because one of their number had been instrumental in saving it from destruction centuries before.

The children arrived on a day marred by dismal weather and instead of being able to properly explore the Abbey and the hidden treasures of the courtyard, they spent the day inside. They could hear the clamouring sounds of the city beyond the walls but within the privacy of the court, there was a placid calm. Father Dante himself showed them to their rooms and explained to them the routine of the Abbey. After they settled their backpacks on the floor by their beds, they met in the cold stone passageway.

"I wonder where Sigil is, we haven't seen him at all since we've been here," said Solomon. Mara shrugged and pattered down the hallway to look at the paintings on the walls. "Don't run off Mara, I might not be able to find you if you wander too far." He followed her and, in a moment, they were standing before a tall painting that was positioned on the wall far above their heads. Both of them had to lean back to fit the entire thing into their view. The painting was of a beautiful girl, dressed in white, her face a vision of melancholy.

Mara held her breath for a moment as she took the painting in. "She's sad," she said, stepping back slightly. "I wonder why she's so sad."

Solomon stepped back alongside her and nodded. "She looks kind of mad, too," he said. "Like she didn't want anyone to paint her that day." He looked up and down the length of the hall. "I wonder who she was." After a few quiet moments, they continued on their exploration. There were more paintings and crossed swords and a shield. There were hanging tapestries with scenes from the Bible and other books but there were no electrical lights, only torches or candles burning in sconces on the walls. There was a twisting stairway at the end of the hallway, carved from white marble, seeming to cascade like a chalky waterfall from the ceiling above. It climbed both upwards from where they stood and descended to the floor below. They stood on either side of the banister and peered upward, but from there they couldn't see to to the top. Mara was the first to risk it.

"Mara, wait!" exclaimed Solomon, hurrying to catch up with her. "What if Father Dante wanted us to stay near our rooms?" Neither Sigil nor Father Dante had made any such restrictions but Solomon was cautious in his new surroundings. Looking ahead, he was just able to see the bottoms of Mara's boots as they disappeared around a turn. When he neared the top, he saw that the stairs became a tight passageway with a low ceiling above. He found Mara stretching upward and struggling to open a wooden trap door that was set into the bricked ceiling. He gently moved her out of his way and pushed against the door. It creaked and opened into a spacious room that had enormous windows looking out in every direction. The room was bare of furnishings except for a stand of sticks and swords on one wall, and various musical instruments. Standing in the center of the room, with an impatient look on his face was Father Dante.

"Hurry up, the both of you," he said. "You were not brought here to dawdle. Or to play, although playing is one of the few things that I think you *should* have been brought here to do. Alas, I am not the one who makes those decisions. That is left for a higher authority. I told you two to hurry! You're dawdling!" The children, upon hearing the tone in Father Dante's voice, scrambled up the remaining stairs and nearly tumbled into the room. Father Dante cast a critical eye in their direction, taking in the image of the two children scrambling to their feet, the trap door slamming shut behind them. "Very good, very good. Now, what shall be the first question that I will allow you to ask me?" Both children looked at the floor nervously. The priest had a manner of speaking that was exactly the manner that made children nervous, but the good sort of nervous. Not the sort of nervous that caused children to be frightened, but the sort of nervous that caused excitement.

The three of them walked around the edge of the room looking out of the windows. Solomon held Mara's hand in his as they trailed behind Father Dante. The city sprawled out on all sides, and below them, in the street, they saw signs of war. Soldiers in battle gear, helmeted and vested, marched in formation on every street. There were armored vehicles all aligned and kitted out, and there were hundreds or thousands of frightened people. Mara didn't understand any of it.

"Why are they all scared, Father Dante?" She said his name 'Don-Tay!', in two separate parts, a first *and* a last name.

"They are preparing for a fight, child," he said. "They are preparing for war."

"Why do they want to fight?" she asked, but Father Dante saw that she already knew the answer.

"They don't," he replied, in an even voice, "but they will. It is too late to stop it. The best that we can hope for is that

128

you and your brother can retrieve some of what is lost." She halted, causing Solomon to stop with her.

"How?" she asked.

"That is the very reason that you have been brought to this place. And that is the only reason that your teachers are here. They have been waiting a tremendously long time for the two of you to be ready, and now that you are here, your training must begin."

THE INITIAL STAGES of the conflict were turbulent. At first, there was a frantic restructuring and consolidation of the judicial system throughout the city, resulting in the formation of the officially titled Judicial Branch. Those citizens who resisted were harshly controlled; small skirmishes became common and rapidly grew into larger riots and anti-Judicial actions. As the fighting escalated outside the walls of the chapel, the children grew, both in stature and ability. The first year, they often saw Sigil. He would return to the chapel and tell them stories about the growing hostilities. As the second year turned to the third, he appeared at the gate of the chapel less and less until finally, he did not return. Father Dante explained to them that only the hazards of the military buildup and the problems that it caused forced him to sometimes stay away. Mara was always beside herself with joy when she would see him in the courtyard, or in the study with the Father and she was inconsolable when he appeared no longer.

There was an aura about the passageways of the upper floors of the Abbey that permeated the children's lives there. It was not a bad feeling, nothing like a sense of dread, but more a sense of awe, a presence of spirit. A grand and terrible history seemed to seep throughout the halls and chambers of the place and, as though they possessed the power of geomancy, the children felt that the very stones had a tale and a mystery that they concealed within their faded and crumbled mortared joints. Deep within the grain of the rock, there was a story that sat waiting just beyond human awareness as though the stones were gossips that could no longer hold their tongues and withhold their secret any longer. It seemed that the children had brought this torrent to the fore and it was now ripe to be spilled. The monks gathered it into their own lives and carried a new anxiety with them on their daily tasks of prayer. Although they loved the children greatly, they could not help but feel worried about the troubles that had been uncovered. Father Dante had issued strict orders that the monks were not to let the children know just how much their presence had disrupted the chapel routine and so they were treated as if their arrival at the chapel was nothing less than a gift from God.

ONE EVENING, as the daylight faded in the passages in the Abbey, Mara stood and pondered the portrait of the sorrowful girl that hung in the hall outside her room. In the two years that she had studied in the Abbey, she had walked by it many times and it constantly called her to return her thoughts to it. Now she stood beneath the flickering light of the torches that bracketed it, and stared at the picture. The girl's eyes seemed to bore into the child's and to draw her ever closer to the faded canvas and ancient gilded frame. Mara blinked and tore her eyes away from the girl and took a breath.

"I remember you..." she whispered, and her hand reached out to the girl but the frame was far up the wall, beyond her reach. She shook the enchantment from her eyes and dropped her hand to her side. After a moment, she came to a decision and suddenly turned and shuffled in her slippers back to her room, her nightdress swishing. She reemerged from her doorway with Brownie in one hand and dragging a wooden chair behind her. She tugged at the chair until it was directly beneath the portrait and then she arranged it neatly against the wall. Clutching her bear tightly, she climbed on her knees onto the chair and then balanced on her toes till she could reach the face of the girl in the picture. She moved her hand across the texture of the paint, feeling the rough canvas beneath it. She felt each brushstroke as if she had held the brush in her own hand and had studied the face of the saddened girl, trying to express the melancholy and sorrow that shrouded her eyes. Mara closed her eyes and spread her arms to touch the frame on either side of the portrait, and then she brought her hand back to the face of the girl. "I remember you," she repeated, "and you remember me." She opened her eyes and stared into the eyes of the girl. For a long moment, Mara was still. Then she suddenly brought her free hand straight up to the top of the frame and with her tiny form fully extended, she ran her hand along the top edge of the portrait. With a rustling noise, a tattered parchment slid from the edge of the frame and slithered to the stone floor beneath her.

Mara twisted to see where it had gone and realized that it had settled directly beneath her chair. She spun around and crouched down to sit on the chair and hung her head between her legs to seek the scrap of parchment. She stretched her hand to reach it and scrambled off of the chair to finally put her hand around it. She looked back up at the girl in the picture as if to say *'I knew that you had something for me'* and slowly, carefully unfolded the parchment. Written in an elegant hand across the aged page was a long verse. Mara saw the ancient script and recognized the line as Angelic script that she had learned from Father Dante. She sat in the wooden chair and began to read.

I had a bad dream on my way up the stairs
A sign of foreboding, a feeling of dread.
I felt I had seen this unfolding beforehand;
Not heeding this warning, I forged on ahead.
Onward and upward, forever ascending,
My footfalls determined on spiraling steps.
A facade of bravado, courageous pretending
For when I first saw it, my heart simply wept.

I saw a grim figure, hidden, enshrouded.
A man or a woman? I could not discern
A veil of linen occluded its features,
I knew at that moment I could not return.
My one point of origin forever denied me,
I held firm resolve, It beckoned me close.
I stared, apprehensive, down into the stairwell,
My only escape from that terrible ghost.

The Abbey

But my recent path was none too inviting,
Just a dismal abyss, Where were the stairs?
Gone, and what was quite adequate lighting
Had dimmed and distorted, thus doubling my fears.
I shifted my gaze back up toward the spectre,
Looking more closely, in spite of my fright.
Upon second glance, disturbing me, troubling me,
I saw what was truly a heartrending sight.

The vision's ill will was not as pronounced
As my initial inspection had shown.
In fact, as I moved a bit closer to It,
I realized that It had some fear of It's own.
It was a young damsel, a shivering maiden
Her cloak with its hood had served to disguise
A delicate beauty, so fragile yet haunting,
It seemed that the light had played tricks on my eyes.

Her face had a look of such desolation
A sadness, as though she'd abandoned all thought
Of ever dispelling the gripping vexation
That clouded her visage, She was so distraught.
I wanted to grant her some slight consolation,
To comfort this creature was now my sole aim.
My thoughts of caution and my trepidation
Were shrinking away when she whispered my name.

My shock was complete for she could not have known me.
A woman so striking I'd surely recall
But then came again, that same dreadful feeling
That gripped me so tightly as I left the hall.
A feeling of slipping, of falling or tripping
With nothing to cling to, nothing to hold
She held out her hand and I had a vision
Of things from the past, of things that are old.

Her voice, like a fragrance, had triggered these memories,
Brought the sensation of once having been
There on that stairway, standing before her,
Hearing her call me, the question was when?
When had I been there? How did she know me?
Was I in some way the cause of her pain?
She addressed me once more, her tone was accusing,
I now was quite certain that I was insane.

My thinking was fuzzy, my reasoning addled,
No other story could I make to fit
The mystical nature of this strange occurrence,
To see her, to know her, and then to forget.
I ransacked and plundered the rooms of my history,
Sorted and sifted and lifted the rug
Under which I might have swept such a mystery
Deeper and deeper and deeper I dug

Into the burial ground I held sacred
In peace far too long had these skeletons slept
Each of their graves an elaborate pitfall,
Traps into which I'd so fatefully stepped
The web of my youth had so tightly ensnared me
But so far the spider had yet to take shape
This girl and her vague anonymity dared me
To answer her challenge, or make my escape.

Before I could speak though, or make any action
She moved and my face felt the touch of her hands,
Then she embraced me, soft as a shadow
Her arms made a necklace of gossamer strands
Her lips touched my own and I tasted a sweetness
A lightness of spirit, as though I'd been blessed
By the very first touch of this sad little angel.
Then I felt her heart through the swell of her breast.

The Abbey

It beat like a kitten's, when frightened and trembling,
It's pulled from its litter and left on its own.
Each beat felt to me as though it were the last one
The panic this caused chilled me straight to the bone.
To find her and then in that moment to lose her
A crueler injustice, I could not devise
For you see, when she held me and then when she kissed me
It seemed as if blindness had fled from my eyes

I now saw her face with full recognition
The haze that had clouded my mind had dispersed
Her's was the image I'd offered my soul to,
But my vow to her had been tragically cursed.
Ours was a pact made in haste and in passion
Tinted by lust and impetuous youth
And like many promises made in that fashion
It did not become the eventual truth.

I thought I'd not see her again in my lifetime
My single true love, irretrievably lost.
The thread of my life had unwrapped and unraveled
And through all my travels our paths had not crossed
It took just three things, her body so frail,
The choke of her breath and the sting of her tears
To conjure up demons of jealous betrayal
There on that stairway, on those wicked stairs.

The love that she gave was a squandered possession
My brutal acts would result in her shame.
I'd prayed for this chance to reverse my transgression
To beg her forgiveness, that I might reclaim
Her love for my own, but my time was so fleeting,
I feared she might vanish as quick as she'd come.
I felt then between us the slow mournful beating
Of my heart alone like some funeral drum.

She'd faded as if she could sense my intention
My slumber had ended and so it would seem
That our final embrace was my mind's own invention
She was never my love, She was simply my Dream.

When she had finished the poem, Mara paused and a tear fell from her eye. She felt the years of loss and sadness in the very page that she held in her hand. The emotions were beyond her years and so she could only understand them in a very simple and powerful way, for there were no complications or evasions to cloud her vision of the girl on the stair. She saw the story unfold in her mind's eye and she felt the agitation of the pen itself as it had traced the words across the page. As she held the parchment to her, with her back to the wall on which the portrait hung, she did not see the figure that was standing in the passageway watching as she wept. She was startled by the scrape of a boot on the stone and looked up to see Sigil standing before her.

"Oh! You're home!" she exclaimed and ran to embrace him and he picked her up and held her out in front of him. Her eyes shone with excitement as she forgot the poem and the portrait of the girl and instead focused on Sigil. "We missed you, Sigil," she said.

"You're much bigger than last time, Mara. You'll soon be too heavy for me," he said. He noticed the parchment grasped in her hand. "What is that that you were reading, child?" He let her down to the floor and held out his hand. "It seems that I may have seen that before." She looked down sadly at the parchment and held it out to him.

"It's a poem," she said. "About the girl in the painting, I think. I think something very bad happened to her, something to hurt her heart." Sigil took the poem from her and folded it carefully. Then he reached up and replaced it atop the painting's frame. He turned and sat heavily in the chair beneath the painting, arranging Mara on his lap and she arranging Brownie on hers.

He then spoke in answer to Mara's questioning face. "You are right, child. Something bad did happen to her, and I was the cause of it. I was the author of that poem." He saw the surprise and distress that was apparent on her face, for she couldn't stand to imagine that Sigil would have felt the sadness that she could sense from those words.

Chapter 14

War

THE FIGHTING wore on. In a race against the Judicial forces and their sympathizers, the monks of the Abbey were secretly sent into the city to locate and procure any and all works of art and literature. The monks had spent many years developing an underground system of tunnels that led from isolated regions of the city into the Abbey. To avoid detection, many of the tunnels had been laced with explosive charges and were destroyed in clashes with units of Judicial soldiers. Many brothers of the Order died in the tunnels and Mara and Solomon would sometimes see certain monks one day and then never see them in the Abbey again. Their education continued uninterrupted but Father Dante did not hide the ravages of war from them. There were services in the chapel for fallen brothers and both of the children were called on to assist the refugees and the wounded that were sometimes given asylum and shelter inside the Abbey. Although they were seldom permitted to leave the grounds of the courtyard, much of their schooling and training revolved around the war.

In addition to spiritual training, Father Dante spent many long hours speaking to them about the history of the Abbey and of how he had become the Abbot there.

"I was always religious in temperament," he began, "but I was atheistic." He saw the uncomprehending looks on their faces. "I did not believe in anything that I could not see with my own two eyes." They sat under a tree in the courtyard of the Abbey and watched as the birds flocked and settled into the branches above them. "I had hopes though. I wanted to believe. In anything that was beyond The World. As a boy, I was led to believe all manner of foolishness and, as a result, I became resistant to credulity." He noticed once again that he had used a word that the children did not know. He spoke in an exasperated tone. "I wanted *proof.* You both know that there is an extensive library in this church. You cannot expect me to explain every word I use to you. I am not your literature instructor! Try to keep up!" He went on. "Now, where was I? Oh, yes. I required proof. I embarked on a path of study that led me away from the church and into a life of crime and that was where I met your friend Sigil. He was also leading a life of adventure that was far away from the teachings of Rome. We met when we had both decided to steal the same thing. A book. We had both developed an interest in old and valuable books."

He flashed a sharp look at the children, who were fidgeting and appeared to find the local wildlife more interesting than the tale that he was relating. "Mara! Pay attention!" he scolded. "This does concern the both of you. Why I was chosen to guide such undisciplined children, I will never know. Ahhh, but we all have our crosses to bear, or so I am told. What was I saying again? Right. Books. Old books. Yes. Sigil and I had been looking for a particular book, one that we both thought would explain exactly why some of the things that we couldn't believe, seemed to be very familiar to us. It had been something that had plagued me my whole life. I couldn't force myself to believe in religion and I thought it was because it was so implausible. Later in my life, I realized that it was not because the ideas of religion were unbelievable that I could not accept them, but rather that the ideas of religion were actually memories that I had forgotten. Sort of like asking someone to believe in their house. You see? People like us don't believe in religion, children. People like us *are* religion. My research had led me to one particular book that contained the words and music to a piece called The Litany of Stars. Your friend Sigil was looking for it as well, and we decided to join forces, so to speak."

At the mention of the book, Mara seemed to look more intently at Father Dante. Her expression became one of open curiosity. The priest continued, "The search for the book led us to this Abbey, and it was here that I took my vows. I have been here ever since." He looked lovingly at the walls and steeple of the courtyard and chapel. "This has been my home and calling and it has showed me my place in the celestial story." His eyes darkened. "This place is something more to Sigil though, he knew it from a time before." His eyes cleared and he looked at the children and began to rouse them. "Up, up, we can't dally here all day. We have work to do today. The life of a monk is full of both grace and labor. You may not be monks, but you still have a calling, both of you. We have wasted enough time dawdling, now up, up, up and back inside the chapel."

THE BELLS THAT RANG for the Morning Prayer would awaken Solomon each morning. Dante, who waited by the door of his room, would greet him and together they would walk the length of the passageway and ascend the marble stairway that led to the chamber above. Once within the chamber, Solomon's training would begin. It was the same every day. Solomon would learn by rote the glyphs and symbols that he would trace in the air, he was taught the difficult phrases that made up the magical lexicon and, all the while, Dante would lecture to him about the intricacies of strategy, or history or theology. Solomon wrapped his fingers around the form that was invisible beyond his mind's eye and shaped it like clay into a newer, more personal form. The form that he imagined was to become the vessel for the spell that he would weave. Once the vessel was created in his mind, he would use his voice to pour the spell into it. Dante was a strict taskmaster and he demanded nothing less than perfection in the execution of spells. There were various advanced techniques and, as the months wore on, Solomon was introduced to greater degrees of magic. There were spells and invocations that were created through subtle movements of the hands or arms and there were rituals that resembled dances that would conjure arcane forces. Solomon was introduced to them all.

Dante would incessantly inspect his room and his attire because he felt that cleanliness was a sign of mental purity and encouraged clarity of thought. The young boy was expected to exercise and perform absolution with the monks of the Abbey and they were spartan in their discipline. The chores of the Abbey were another requirement and Solomon cleaned the scullery and the dining hall daily.

Around the Abbey, the tension boiled and churned and Solomon could hear the reports of gunfire and the thud of shells throughout the day and night. The only reprieve from the seemingly relentless regimen came when Sigil would return. Then, there would be a special dinner and Solomon and Mara would sit on either side of him as he would tell stories of the war and of the battles with the Judicial forces. Solomon imagined what it must be like to face a Judicial soldier and he was afraid. The soldiers were sent by his father and he knew that his father had tried to kill Mara. But he remembered that Sigil had told him that his father had wanted him to live. He wondered if the soldiers would try to kill him.

ONCE, when Solomon had just completed a particularly difficult series of exercises, Father Dante seemed to retreat into a state of remembering. He became more talkative than usual, and began to relate the tale of the Fall, and of the origin of The Order of Dismas.

"The legend grows in the telling. The history of The Order of Dismas is shrouded in secrecy. Founded in the deserts of the Middle East and Northern Africa, our teachings stretch historically into Asia, Europe and the Americas. References to our ideas surface in ancient Buddhist scripts, Chinese strategic studies and Greek mathematical and philosophical texts. They were found in the writings of early European alchemists and in the discoveries of modern physicists.

"In the early years, when mankind was still in its infancy, the magical races had settled on Earth, exiled from their original homes amongst the stars. They were fugitives, fleeing from a defeat and from a narrow escape. The defeat was at the hands of a great power, greater than any that man has ever known, and the escape was narrow enough to whittle them to just a small fraction of their original number. These people of the stars were not material in body, they were created of light and finer stuff and when they approached the Earth, they spied the ape-like creatures that populated the land."

He paused to look sternly at Solomon and to make a slight correction in the boy's form. He went on. "Still stinging from their recent defeat and wounded in pride and body, they felt compelled to possess these apes and make the animal's bodies their own. Against the will of the apes, and also against the will of their own leaders, many of the people of the stars inhabited the bodies and minds of the simple apes and began to use them as playthings. The greater minds and souls among them refused to indulge in such things and admonished their crueler cousins, reminding them that it was cruelty and arrogance that had led to their banishment and the loss of their place in the sky, but the wicked ones were adamant, insisting that it was their due, reasoning that if they were to be cast from their former splendor in the heavens, then they should at least have slaves and entertainment in their material prison. In time the star-people forgot that they were beings of light, and in their forgetfulness they became entranced by the bodies of the apes. They fell under the spell of the hunger and the anger, and of the pain and the pleasure that the apes could receive."

Solomon finished the exercise and waited for Dante's dismissal. The priest waved him to a corner and gestured to him to take a seat on the floor while he continued with the lecture. "They began to create their own drama, using the bodies of the apes for their theater. Their only passion was for experience, and since they could not die in the physical sense, they craved things that were inherently harmful. These star-people had little concern for the freedom of their simian hosts, and even less for their bodies. Tossing aside the lives of the animals like the discarded shells of nuts, they would move on to greater and greater depravities at the expense of the innocent apes. It was never enough to simply enjoy the earthly pleasure of food or drink, or the satisfaction of labor or love. It was always an insatiable groping for lust and violence, power and competition.

"The star-people eventually forgot their astral origins so completely in order to more fully experience the pathos and trials of mortality, that they became convinced that they were the apes themselves. They began partaking in the breeding of the animals, a crime that their leaders could never forgive nor absolve them from. The minds of the apes continued to develop alongside the star-people, both spirits inhabiting the same flesh, melding together, forming as one soul, growing into a strange and frightened creature. A creature terrified and confused at the opposition inside of it, forever sensing, painfully and eternally aware of the high estate from which it has fallen, but condemned to be pulled to the earth by the instinctive anchor of its race.

"All beings that live on this green earth are descendants of this blasphemy, and we grapple with that and all that it entails every moment of our short, wicked lives. This is why all that we crave is dangerous for us, and we will always hurt every single being who loves us. The great cults and temples all teach us to fear pleasure and to seek pain and sacrifice and this is because of the ancient and nearly forgotten memory of our ancestry."

The priest paused for a moment and removed a rosary from within the folds of his robe. Making the sign of the cross, he fingered the prayer beads absently. Solomon recognized the gesture and the beads as memory aids, mnemonics to assist in focusing power. He waited patiently until Father Dante continued. "We have been reminded of the truth, time and time again, in the teachings of the Kristos and the avatars, and in our hard and blackened souls we know that these things are true. We are exiled here and have welcomed death instead of immortality so that we can feel what its like to die, again and again. It is the single saddest tale in the cosmos, a tragedy that has no equal on any level of imagination. We stay in this prison that kills us because we are afraid of a cold nothingness in the stars. We cannot flee our destiny, Solomon, we must all face our birth and our duty to our celestial family. We may have forgotten our angelic cousins, but they have never forgotten us."

Solomon felt a twinge of strange regret at this last remark. Father Dante saw his expression and spoke with more force; he warmed to his subject. "We still have a chance to escape the event loop; it is possible for a man or woman to seek reality beyond the physical, to study the forces that exist in higher realms. These forces are evident in manifestations of higher energies that people utilize in their technologies. These vibrational patterns set up resonant matrices that are the real energies around you. Not the physical stuff that the matrix describes but the blueprint of the relationship, understand?" He aimed a stern look at Solomon, implying that he wasn't paying close enough attention. "To take the architectural metaphor further, not the building itself, but the design of the building. The mathematical descriptors of the processes in this environment are the carriers of the wave, not the air or the water or any particular medium. All of it is consciousness, and easily manipulated by faith or will. The evil among us use will, the most holy among us use faith. It is our intent to train you to be able to do these things, to change this frame of reference for yourself and for the others around you. Our order has existed for centuries on this plane, waiting for the first of our brothers to awaken from their self-induced slumber and repent their sins. I have been waiting to take you on as a student. We must work quickly though; your movement through the astral web and your recent return to the Earth has been recorded. The ancient enemy has been watching with no small amount of interest and we can be sure that he has dispatched his agents to intercept you." With that final, ominous pronouncement, Father Dante brought his attention back to his student. He suddenly remembered that Solomon had been sitting silently, waiting. He absentmindedly waved his hand, gesturing that the boy was dismissed for the day and turned away as Solomon rose to his feet and prepared to leave.

As an afterthought, he paused and turned back to his young student. "We realize that all of this is confusing for you, Solomon. You must have faith. It is truly the only protection that may remain for you and your sister." Solomon hesitated and then, bowing his head just slightly to his instructor, he turned and left the chamber.

ON SPECIAL DAYS, Solomon would sometimes be allowed to accompany Father Dante on small errands into the city. The child walked slightly out of step with the older, graying man at his side. They moved through the crowded city, slipping through the multitude of humanity that made up The World. The boy would follow the aged priest through the teeming crowds and wonder at the sad people that he saw in the streets. In every face, he saw recent tears and he somehow knew that his father was responsible. This made him feel as though he was responsible as well. There were Judicial Troopers on every corner, their weapons at the ready and leveling stares of intimidation at the populace.

On one such occasion, they found themselves at a hardly noticeable door just as the last remnants of daylight were fading. Dante removed his cloak and beckoned to the boy and they both entered a shabby dwelling that bordered the cobblestone walkway. Once inside, Solomon realized that they were not alone and that there were many others inside, seated around a huge wooden table. The room was much bigger on the inside than it seemed from the outside and a glowing orange fire cast a somber, reddish glow over the assembled faces.

A monk that was clad in the same sort of robe that Father Dante and the monks of the Abbey wore was standing on the near side of the table and he was speaking in a low voice. "From where do we come? Are we an order of spies or assassins, a thieves guild or criminal cartel, a secret society or conspiracy, revolutionary heroes or simply a myth? What say you? Do any of you know the truth of our order's history?"

He looked about the room, at the upturned faces of the other monks crowded around the table. He turned his head and nodded at Father Dante and Solomon as they entered the room behind him. He raised his voice and continued. "Some say that a few men from military institutions or the intelligence community, disillusioned with their employers, created their own "spy school". Other tales point to a secretive group of adventurers and researchers, stumbling upon forbidden knowledge, passed it along to those students whom they most trusted. Still others claim it is just an advanced, highly complex way to study a martial art. The oddest thing about these rumors and anecdotes is that none of them actually come from a member of their group or anyone who studied with them."

The monk laughed a short laugh, looking at the new arrivals. He leaned lower, and spoke distinctly to Solomon. "When Christ was crucified, the man who was hung on the right side of Our Lord was named Dismas. He repented at the very last and begged God for forgiveness. He is known as the good thief. The Order is named for him; he is the patron saint of thieves. Learn your trade well boy, in this line of work it is not out of the realm of imagination that you could end up just like him."

"A saint?" asked Solomon.

"No...crucified," replied the monk.

THERE WAS A NIGHT, after he had returned and the evening meal was completed, when Sigil found Solomon seated by himself on the floor in the training chamber. He approached the boy in the darkened room and sat at his right side, facing him at a right angle. This was the accustomed position for a teacher to address a student as it allowed Sigil to see Solomon clearly while Solomon could not face him directly.

"I've noticed that your training has advanced beyond the fifth degree," he said. He gestured at the instruments and weapons arrayed on the racks that circled the chamber. "Soon you will need no tools at all. Your mind will be your instrument." He saw Solomon's expression change slightly and he spoke again. "Is there something wrong, Solomon, something you wish to speak about?" Solomon shifted in the kneeling position and looked at the floor, he knew there was no use in attempting to hide his emotions, Sigil was an adept as well and could easily read his tension.

As Solomon spoke, Sigil noticed the tremor in his voice. "Mara doesn't train like I do," he began, "she doesn't *work* like I do." Sigil heard the anger that sat just below the surface of Solomon's words. He studied the boy's face. "She doesn't need the instruments. She never has, not since we came here. All she has to do is think and the spell is cast. It's not fair." Sigil sat quietly for a moment, considering his answer.

"There are things about your sister that are beyond even my understanding or that of Father Dante," he said. "Your powers grow every day, Solomon, more quickly than any student that has ever been trained by the Order. But Mara is beyond training. She has never been taught or guided since she has been here and her abilities are becoming a concern to the Order."

Solomon turned to face Sigil. "What does that mean? How is she a concern?" Sigil could see that beneath the envy that Solomon carried inside of him, there was a deeper sense of protectiveness that came to the fore when he sensed that Mara might be in danger. He recognized the envy immediately and with it he sensed the wounded pride. For the boy to be bested by his younger, female sibling was a sour pill to swallow. Sigil sensed an impending doom.

He answered, trying to soften the meaning behind his words. "She is powerful, Solomon. Yet she is still a small child. Her mind is innocent and she has not yet developed the anger that you or I have. The Order doesn't know what to make of her. They do not like to feel helpless." Solomon looked at Sigil from the corner of his eye; he brought himself back under control and brought his gaze back forward.

Without shifting his position, he spoke a question, "Why are we not training the people of the city? If it is impossible to stop the Judicial attack, then why are we not preparing the people for their defense?" He focused his eyes on a spot on the wall and kept them there.

Sigil thought for a long moment and then replied in slow, measured tones, "It seems, Solomon, that it is human nature to be attracted to the familiar, even if it is uncomfortable. The hunger that the mind has for information about what will happen next, or soon, seems unappeasable. People appear needy to *know* what will happen to them, in order to plan for it. If that information is not available, they will often create it out of a powerful desire. Sometimes, this desire makes them think irrationally. They lie to themselves, or make assumptions to confirm what they believe must happen. This occurs at a dramatically severe level sometimes. I am starting to believe that the people of the cities are creating a false reality for themselves on an individual basis, determined by what their limited perceptions allow them to believe. I think that they actually cannot see the danger that is growing right before their eyes." His eyes lowered and he shook his head sadly. "There have been many writings devoted to this phenomenon. And for mankind's destiny, the implications of this are staggering."

Solomon's expression was cold. He tightened his jaw and spoke in a quiet murmur, almost to himself. "I hate it," he said with an air of disgusted finality. "They're frightened and hopeful at the same time. They're greedy and selfish, but sometimes give in charity. Their upbringing and environment all filter what they can accept as true, and they twist the truth until it becomes what they want. It seems so pathetic, so limiting."

Sigil nodded and narrowed his eyes. He was impressed with Solomon's insight, but wary of the harshness of his tone. "And confusing," he answered. "At the very foundation of it, that idea seems counter-intuitive and yet easily provable. What do you do with an idea like that? It very nearly is the definition of insanity, no? To create your own reality based on your desires? In an insane world, it would seem like the only option is to act insane. Or you can exercise control."

Sigil thought back to the long hours and endless days of his own training, to the countless philosophical discussions of combat and technique. He would sit at the feet of the instructors, men and women who, for countless generations had recorded the exploits of the Order and had pieced together fragments of a doctrine.

"One form of control that should be examined is the technique of only allowing the target to be aware of a finite number of options."

In his memory, Sigil's instructors spoke in dignified tones as they discussed the psychology of control. *"Control is exerted through designing those options and 'feeding' them to the target. A hungry opponent will eat what he is fed. In this way one predicts the defeat of his enemy."*

The next ancient monk spoke in reply, *"How many people must know a secret to stop it from being a secret? A secret is simply knowledge that very few are aware of. Knowledge loses power whenever more people know it, and inversely, gains power when fewer people know it. Not only should one strive to keep knowledge secret, but also to deny that it even exists. The opponent should not know what you know or that you know it."*

The old monk spread a sly grin. *"For example, if one were to procure a key to an opponent's house, one should not steal it, but duplicate it. The opponent should not know that the second key exists. He should not know that you exist. If possible, steps should be taken so that he does not know that the door exists."*

The monk turned his attention to the weary student who was seated next to him. *"Ideally, the target should execute himself and do your bidding for you. He is the one enemy he does not expect, after that his closest allies. He cannot fight himself or an enemy he is not aware of. He must be reactive, never proactive. He must believe the path that leads to his demise is the path to his victory and that he is choosing it of his own accord. It is important to note that you cannot leave your opponent ignorant. He must be extremely knowledgeable and informed, but only with the knowledge that you have 'taught' him."*

Sigil thought about the ways and methods that had been used throughout the centuries to protect the secrets of the Order and wondered if this was the best way to train the child. He looked at the boy kneeling before him and realized how little they really knew. Although he possessed a higher awareness than mankind, he still was beneath both Mara and Solomon. He was sure that the children did not know this. If the very nature of the Order was deceptive, then how could the boy be driven onto the right hand path? Sigil knew, from bitter memory, that lies simply fed and fueled more lies. He knew that the boy's training was tainted, as was his, and that there would be a day of atonement for them all.

SIGIL ADJUSTED Solomon's hands and arranged them into various uncomfortable and exotic positions. Outwardly, it appeared as if the boy was in prayer or performing religious rituals. Solomon, deep in concentration, would remain focused on the symbols that his hands traced in the air, visualizing the final result that he sought. Sweat poured down his face and his muscles trembled but he would hold the positions for hours at times.

This strict discipline was enforced not by threat of punishment but by the words that Sigil spoke in a clear, steady voice as he circled and inspected Solomon's technique. "Why is there no formalized school of fighting? Not of organized warfare or of classical unarmed combat, but of realistic fighting. First, we must define fighting. 'To impose one's will upon the enemy', is one definition. We have military schools, which concern themselves with mass strategy and command, and martial arts styles, which teach archaic forms. What about creating warriors? 'To subdue the enemy without fighting is the pinnacle of a General's skill.' Sun Tzu. Think about that. The actual goal of war is peace. This contradiction is what all warriors face and struggle with. What we are really concerned with is control. Control of our opponent and ourselves. We control our opponent through our ability to control our weapons, our troops, and our bodies.

"Ultimately, we do this with our minds. To train an individual fighter, we must focus on the mind. Why does no martial-arts style train in surveillance or counter-surveillance? A military unit would be crippled without reconaissance assets. One must study your enemy to defeat him. Why don't martial-arts schools teach firearms? Or lock picking? Or cryptography? Why not poisons or driving? Because they are not concerned with the real elements of combat. They focus only on one part of one type of fight. To destroy your enemy, one must be where he thinks you are not, to strike where he does not expect, in a way that he cannot comprehend. He should not even be aware that he has been attacked. Why do all military units have extensive communications capability and train in ambush, yet you could not find a school of fighting that would train the individual to fight this way? Why is there no training in explosives or camouflage?

"You are not a warrior if you do not know these subjects. The topics are endless that a warrior must master. Navigation, mountaineering, computer science, electronics, medicine are just a few. Who trains like this? Is it even possible to learn all of it? Probably not, but it is an ideal to strive for. Only through knowledge of the world comes self-knowledge, and only through self-knowledge comes control. Through control comes peace."

The soldier made more minuscule adjustments to the boy's hands and arms. "Defense, Solomon. Do not allow yourself to be killed. Be like smoke."

SOLOMON'S BREATHING was a subject of great concern to Father Dante, and many months were spent on that subject alone. The boy would kneel with his legs tucked beneath him on the unforgiving wooden floor and the priest would count as he slowly and steadily took in oxygen through his nose and released it just as steadily through the space between his tongue and the roof of his mouth. As he released his breath, he would tighten his abdomen and the air would hiss outward like an angry cat. He would push his hands outward toward the symbol that floated in his mind's eye just in front of his chest and draw the symbol with his will. The sun would move across the sky in a burning arch and the relentless training would continue. As the symbol existed in his mind, so the action that the symbol stood for existed in the world. Father Dante taught him that will was the force that The Most High had used to create the universe and that will was the single blessing that he had bestowed upon man. It was this free will that separated man from the animals that were his subjects.

When Solomon asked Father Dante about the animals, the priest's manner became sober and melancholy. "Realize, Solomon, that this will, this freedom of choice is not your birthright. It has been stolen from its rightful owner and we use it at our peril. As long as our will is in concert with The Most High, we become the instruments that he performs his masterpiece with. When we do as your father has, as Sigil has, we sound in discord. We are not as we appear. We are not men of earth. We are creatures of light and sound."

When Solomon heard Father Dante speak of his father, he would force his shoulders down into his stomach and his hips down into his feet, clenching his muscles tightly. He would twist his feet, screwing them into the polished wood of the training chamber and push his hands outward as Father Dante had taught him, and in his mind's eye, he would see the most wicked things.

THEY STOOD BENEATH the trees in the courtyard of the chapel. Solomon was reaching the end of his patience with his instructor's strict lessons.

"Then this magic is nothing more than numbers and shapes. It's not real." Solomon's frustration overflowed and he broke discipline. He relaxed his posture and let out a breath. "What Mara does is real. Not numbers. This isn't real."

"Indeed, Solomon, it is as real as you or I are real," returned Dante. "Or that stone, or that tree there. The fact is that magic is simply an advanced technology, a novel way to program reality, similar to computing. Pythagoras had realized this, as did Newton and Einstein. Many other thinkers and philosophers had touched on it as well. The ability to wield such power comes at a severe penalty though. Most cannot make such sacrifices. To the typical scientist, these skills would appear as if an extra-terrestrial influence was responsible, and that wouldn't be entirely incorrect. The truth would be closer to the fact that even the familiar rifle, or the typewriter, or the automobile are, in actuality, alien to this planet. By this I mean that human consciousness itself is extra-terrestrial. The flesh of the race was born here, but the mind and soul of the human race originated elsewhere. Those members of the original, untainted stock have been monitoring this cycle for many centuries, and have much interest in you, the soldier Sigil, and your sister. The paltry technologies that we of the Order have managed to patch together using the clumsy hands and tools that are native to these ape bodies are nothing compared to what we are truly capable of. You must fulfill the prophecy, Solomon; you must create the conditions that will allow The Most High to intervene on our behalf. We must escape this planet, and the children are the only way."

"I will try, Father."

"No, Solomon! This must be accomplished! There is no other way! The greater angels have contacted advanced members of the Order, the superior adepts that have broken away from the constraints of the body, and they have spoken of their requirements. You were spoken of by name. By name, Solomon! It is both a supreme honor and horror together. And you cannot refuse, nor can you fail."

"If it is all simple spatial geometry, then there is nothing personal about magic…there are no truly higher beings then? I cannot have reverence for an equation." Solomon's voice had an edge of scorn. He looked into the eyes of the older man and sifted through his memory. There were countless names and invocations that the boy had spent months memorizing, he had studied the scriptures and sutras relating to the Litany of Stars many times but he could not, could never, believe.

The master regarded his student thoughtfully and tried to imagine what the boy would one day become. The answer was all too clear to someone who had spent as many years in study as he had. He knew what Solomon was and he knew also who was responsible. He was afraid for his own soul and had a more realistic notion of "higher beings" than Solomon possibly could. He was aware of the price that Solomon would soon pay.

Only once during his time at the Abbey did Solomon ask Father Dante about his father. The old priest sighed and his lips tightened as he felt the tension rise in the child. He looked at the boy and realized that what he was about to say would change him forever. He forged ahead.

"Nothing on this green earth was more important than himself, nothing was more precious than power. To your father, mathematics was something both tangible and intangible, yet his analytical mind could grasp it. What he could not grasp, would never accept was *purpose*. He couldn't understand that The Most High would expend the energy to create such a beautiful thing as this Earth and then abandon it to the likes of us. His greatest error was holding such a low standard of beauty. The worlds that we come from are infinitely greater than this one, not because this is a particularly ugly world, but because you peek at it through such a small and filthy lens. There are more than three dimensions, obviously, and there are more than five senses, infinitely more. So, this world is not characterized by beauty but by limitation. Think of a photograph of a meal that you could never eat or smell, and you will get some idea of why some view this world as Hell.

"The adepts of this order are just men, not angels or devils, not monsters or heroes. They are fulfilling the roles that the creator has specified for them, no more, no less. Yet, they have no idea what those roles are or how they fit into the grand scheme of things. They have faith. Even the evil ones have faith of a sort, because they believe they will rise to power. Even that implies more faith than that of the apathetic. They at least know that they will have something in the future. The apathetic and atheistic don't even believe in a future. How can you accomplish anything if you cannot see potentiality? That is the worst part of the Descent, the ones who have truly gone native. Lifetime after lifetime of sheer despondency, living like animals but worse. Animals are exactly what God intended for this little slice of Paradise and so they are exactly where they need to be. Angels don't belong here and every second spent here is a second spent in disobedience. There are no good or evil angels, no demons. There are only angels that are forever singing His praises, and then there are the rest of us."

Chapter 15

The Patrol

*Of the return of Thomas Worth
and of a dangerous battle*

"THE CHILD'S abilities have not been honed, there is much more that could be refined in her. They both must stay in the charge of the Order until this war is over. There is too much we don't understand about what Thomas Worth has done to bring her into this world." Sigil leaned forward as he spoke. "The ritual is still hidden behind a veil of incomprehensible glyphs. At best, we are still many years from fully understanding it." He spoke in a calm voice, a counterpoint to the urgency that was creeping into Dante's tone.

"We do not have many years!" replied the priest. "The conflict is upon us now, here. As we speak, aircraft are deploying to strategic targets that will not survive the initial strikes. But the true war is being fought in secret, over intellectual targets. Who would have guessed that it would have come down to this? To the simple things that we overlooked. To things as childlike as the melody contained within a song. If we are unable to discover Worth's technique of invocation, then we have little chance of saving the girl or her brother. Their very souls are at stake and, just when you are needed, you are nowhere to be found."

They sat at the long wooden table in the kitchen of the Abbey and waited as the novices cleared the dishes and cutlery away. When the last of the monks had finished their tasks, Sigil leaned back on his stool and put his hands on the back of his head.

The priest stroked his chin and fixed a stern gaze on the other man. "They both are in a particularly dangerous position, Sigil. You should not stay away from the chapel for so long. Their security is weakened and diminished when you are not here." Sigil looked away for a brief moment, as if he didn't wish to acknowledge the older man's statement.

His eyes returned to the priest. "I know that their father is seeking them, Dante. I know that he will eventually find them here. Did you really believe that they were ever truly safe here? This was nothing more than an effort to buy us time, a gambit to give us room to breathe, nothing more."

Father Dante's irritation was evident. His voice rose in volume, and he struggled to bring it back under control.

"We have done all that we could to train and educate them, to prepare them both for the day that Thomas Worth would seek them out, but the girl was unteachable. There has been no technique that was effective. She was simply beyond every disciple here." He pursed his lips and shifted in his seat. He gripped the edge of the table and there was an obvious tension that Sigil could feel vibrating through the wood. "I, and the rest of the brothers of the Order, fear for her life." He paused and then went on. "I fear for her very soul."

Sigil nodded slowly and considered his words before he spoke. "The boy is at a greater risk, he is troubled within. He does not know it but he may have been the true reason that his father performed the ritual. Don't forget, Dante, that I have dealt with his father many times before." He toyed with the candle that had been placed on the table and thought of the children. The situation weighed heavily on his mind. "There is no alternative to the operations outside of the Abbey. The volunteers that I have been able to scour from the city are incapable of working on their own for any realistic amount of time. They are untrained and frightened. We cannot ease the pressure now."

"I disagree," said Dante. "These military excursions of yours go directly against the charter of this brotherhood. Do not forget that you are first a member of The Order of Dismas, and this is not an order of soldiers!" His expression was heated and a flush of color was in his face. "Our first priority is the will of The Most High! Your true nature seems to be coming to the fore, Sigil, and I will not allow it to harm these children!" He put his palms flat on the table and seemed as if he was about to rise to his feet.

Sigil leaned forward slightly and held the aged priest back with a hard look. "We are *all* soldiers, Father!" he said. "And my true nature is not so different than yours. It's only that I am forced to recall it every day. Blessed is forgetfulness. These are not simple children, and the boy has a more malignant nature than my own. Perhaps a more malignant one than his father's. I can only pray that we overestimate Solomon's willfulness and that we underestimate Mara's power. We will need her power soon. And their father is only one of our concerns."

The priest raised his eyebrows in amazement. "How can you say such things, being a man of God? What could possibly be more important than stopping Thomas Worth from fulfilling this prophecy? Where is your heart?" His lip trembled in anger and his eyebrow twitched.

"This order is a bevy of thieves, Dante. As are they all, and every man is a man of God, in His eyes. Do not allow yourselves to believe your own dogma. The operations that we engage in outside of these walls are the last gasps of a dying world. You must have faith that The Most High will finish his drama in typical high style. Has he ever done otherwise? Without the element of risk, there would not be value in the prize that is gained and until we become comfortable with death, we can never win eternal life. Mara knows this."

The priest sat back on his stool and appeared to deflate slightly. He held his face in his hands and looked toward the ceiling. He seemed to wrestle with the words that the younger man had spilled onto the table before him and his struggle was one that caused him to frown and tighten his face.

After a long moment, he let a slow breath escape from his lips. "It is true that we are nothing but thieves, Sigil. And perhaps we all share in the nature of the Fall. But allowing that creature to use those children is beyond what even this order can accept in faith. We do not share your ability to see through the veil of time and space, and we only know of what the child can see from our research and study. But I tell you this, in spite of her great power, and in spite of her immense destiny, she is still a small child. She still walks through this world with an element of innocence and she deserves as much as any other child. For a time at least. It is not just that she be at the mercy of devils."

He pushed against the table a final time and raised himself slowly to his feet. He brushed the crumbs from his supper from his robe and started to turn to the door of the kitchen. He paused and looked at the gray clad man who sat across the table from him and spoke with great emotion. "There is no one else here in this place who can help them, and she has come to rely on you for guidance. Please, I beg you one last time. Give up this war that you wage, Sigil, and bring these children home." He pulled his brown, woolen hood over his shaven head and stepped into the dark, stone halls of the Abbey.

THE FIRST WAVES of the final Judicial assault came in the dead of night. Judicial Troops converged on major metropolitan areas and occupied any intellectual centers. All forms of free speech were immediately shut down. Universities, television stations, radio, Internet, all were taken within the first hours of the assault. The radicals had already coined the term "Culture War" and it seemed an apt description. Mara was enraged. A deeply rooted sensation of fury washed through her as she saw her beloved Abbey stripped of its treasures. The music and art that she had been immersed in since she and Solomon had left their home was now inaccessible to her. She spent days rewriting from memory, refrains of songs and snatches of nearly forgotten melodies.

Her brother took a more tangible path, choosing instead to engage in acts of vandalism against the Judicials at every turn. Undetected, he would climb a tree in the Abbey garden, disappear over the wall and spend the night breaking or defacing any unattended Judicial property that he could find. He would return sometime after the monks began midnight prayer and before they awoke in the mornings.

The two of them would confer at night about the state of the cities and discuss in hushed tones what they thought should be done, but to no consequence, they were as helpless as the people of the cities. The Judicial occupation continued, and the children and the monks of the Order could do nothing in the face of the onslaught.

THE SMALL BAND of fighters had been moving overland for about five days, narrowly avoiding Judicial patrols the entire way. Sigil walked in the center of the formation, next to a teen-aged boy with a radio antennae extending from his pack. A coiled cord stretched from the radio to the handset that Sigil held. He uttered a terse command into the radio, and then gestured to the younger man and handed him the handset. The boy reattached it to the side of his pack. Motioning silently to the others, Sigil halted and lowered himself slowly to one knee. He reached into the large pocket on his thigh and pulled out a tattered map. As he studied it, one of the others furtively moved from the very front of the formation to where Sigil crouched.

"How is it up there on point?" asked Sigil in a whisper. "Can you see anything at all?"

"It's a little rough in this low light, sir," she replied, pulling the bandanna from her head and wiping the sweat from her forehead. "I guess it's better than them seeing us first though. How much further, sir?" Sigil twisted the map so that she could see the route clearly, and then shone a small red tinted light onto the ragged paper. He cupped his hand over the beam of light, restricting the glare to the surface of the map. The point looked at the map and tapped her index finger on a line that wiggled through its center. "We should be coming to this road soon. If we cut across it, we can cut at least a day off of our march. This would be a lot easier, sir, if I had the map with me."

"I know it would, and I'm sorry for sticking you out there like this. I can only carry one copy of the map and once I leave this escort, you will all be safer if you don't know exactly what my objective is." He looked closely at the road that her finger was resting on. "We can't cross it, we've been extremely lucky so far. That road will be heavily patrolled and we have to arrive at our destination undetected. If you're getting worn out up there, let me know and I can have someone else take point for a while." He folded the map, then returned it to his pocket and rose to his feet.

"I'm good, sir, I have a few more kliks left in me. Thanks though." Her frame bent, she silently disappeared into the twilight. Sigil signaled to the others kneeling in the underbrush around him and they stood and continued walking.

THE GROUP WAS SITUATED on a hillside looking down at a collection of official-looking buildings, surrounded by a menacing barbed-wire fence. Sigil, while remaining prone on the ground, removed his pack and stripped off his extraneous gear. He surveyed the facility with field glasses, searching for anything that could be used to his advantage. There were several heavily armed Judicial soldiers visible, walking patrols inside the fence, and he assumed that there were more somewhere outside the fence as well.

"Here is where I leave you," he said to the point, who was lying in the grass beside him. "I'll finish the rest of this alone."

The point stared through the lenses of her own binos and spoke without looking away, "You know that we'll go in with you sir, you only have to ask." She reached along her side to pull a stone out from beneath her hip, settling back into the shallow trench she had made in the grass. "There are a lot of troops in there."

Sigil shook his head and continued to prepare to leave the band behind, checking his weapon and securing his pack in the underbrush. "I'll be fine, don't worry, I do this sort of thing all the time," he said, rolling back over to his belly. The point finally took her eyes away from the binos and looked at Sigil. After a moment, she set her jaw and turned her face back toward the fenceline.

"Roger that, sir," she said flatly, her eyes screwed tightly into the eyecups of the binos. "You're in charge." Her lips were pursed tightly together and her knuckles were white as she pressed the field glasses into her eyes. "That's a satellite facility, isn't it?" she asked.

"Sorry," replied Sigil, "need to know and all of that, I really can't talk about it." He inspected his kit one final time and, without hesitating, he stood and began his approach toward the fence. Within moments he was out of sight of the point as she lay in the grass, focusing the binos. She continued to watch even when he had disappeared.

Bypassing the fence was a relatively simple task for Sigil; the work that he was to complete once he was inside was considerably more daunting. He crept noiselessly past the turned back of a Judicial sentry as the guard dozed in a standing position. Sigil was relying on the lax attitude of the guards to get him as far as possible into the facility, but he knew that he would eventually be forced to face a more attentive foe. He looked beyond the guard and saw a wide expanse of open and exposed ground between his position and the nearest entrance to the facility and he reasoned that he would have to create an alternative to the traditional way inside. He saw a path, clear and out of the walking pattern of the guards, that would lead him to a section of the building that was hidden from sight nearly to the roof. He quickly traversed it and settled in at the foot of the wall.

With his back pressed against the wall, he could see the hill from which he had recently surveyed the building, and he thought he saw movement there. He waited, out of sight of the guards and of anyone who might see him from the hill. He was concerned that the band of fighters that had escorted him to the objective had been discovered and that his mission had been compromised, so he waited. The movement came again. He squinted in the direction of the movement and reached into the small pouch at his waist and took out his binos. Lifting them to his face, he took the risk of reflecting light back up the hill and took a closer look. Through the lenses, he saw the point staring back at him through her own binos, her chin settled on her arm as it lay in the brush. Sigil frowned and thought quickly, the point was supposed to have left with the others as soon as he had been inserted. He rapidly scanned the area around the point, searching for signs of the rest of the unit. Had there been a problem with their egress? He saw no sign of the fighters but he couldn't risk entering the building until he was aware of what was going on. Without a second thought, he aborted his entry and backtracked along the way he had come. As invisibly as he had moved down the hill, he retraced his steps back to where he had hidden his pack and had lain in the grass. The point was still in the same position as he had left her.

"What are you doing?" he wasted no time in asking her. "Where is the rest of your team?" His voice was stern. "Was there trouble?"

Without looking up at him or removing her eyes from her binos, she answered. "No trouble sir, they left." She refocused the binos and adjusted her elbows in the dirt.

He waited, but when she offered no more details, he spoke again, "Why didn't you leave with them? That was the plan. You made me come back here to check on you. This timeline is blown." His voice was even and calm, but there was a dangerous edge in it, the point could hear the anger just below the calm.

She rolled over to her side and put the binos down. "It's suicide to go in there alone," she said, "I knew you would come back if you saw me. I'm going in there with you." She started to stow her pack in the brush next to his. "Why are you going in there anyway? I mean, why are *we* going in there?" She finished arranging her pack and hefted her weapon. She leveled her gaze at him and waited. He stared at her for a moment and considered his options. He looked at his watch and looked back at the fence that he had just recently crossed twice. He looked back at the point.

"All right," he said, clenching his jaw. "Come on." He motioned for her to go on ahead of him. "It's not as though I have any choice right now. Stay close to me, and stay quiet." She nodded. "Follow my lead exactly, and we may not get killed." They began moving back toward the fence, the point in her accustomed place in the front of the column and Sigil following silently in her wake.

ONCE ON THE ROOF, they crawled on their bellies to a grate that was sealed by a hefty lock. Sigil extracted a small pouch from his pocket and removed a thin metal implement, inserting it into the keyway of the lock. As the lock gave way to his probing, he waved the point through the grate and into the room below. She dropped to the floor and unslung her weapon. She peered into the darkness as Sigil landed, catlike, on the ground next to her. He leveled his rifle in a slow, sweeping arc around the room; she looked up to see the closed grate above them. As he finished his sweep, Sigil noticed her looking upward.

"That's not the way that we're going out," he said. "By the time we leave, they will have begun the patrol of the roof. We'll have to leave by another route." She nodded and followed him to the door.

"Where are we going?" she ventured, cautiously peeking around him as he cracked open the door. A sliver of illumination glanced in from the hallway outside, bathing the room in a sterile, white light.

Sigil spoke without looking back at her, "I'm here to steal a code," he said matter-of-factly, and stepped into the glaring light of the hallway. He beckoned to her to follow and to aim her weapon to the rear. He seemed to know where he was going, so she focused her eyes at a spot in the hall a half-inch above the sights of her weapon. She used her ears to guide her as she shuffled backward, in lockstep with Sigil as he searched. They went past one room and then another, until finally they arrived at a door and Sigil stopped. The metal plate on the door that served as a placard read "Satellite Mainframe Logistics". Motioning to the point to stand post at the entrance, Sigil opened the door and stepped inside. Although it was dark inside the room, a soft light illuminated the screen of a computer terminal, nearly hidden in a corner. The rest of the room was filled with tall racks of server computers, an insistent hum vibrating throughout. Sigil felt the heat that they gave off in spite of the systems that he knew were in place to cool them. He walked to the terminal and sat down, his hands gliding over the keyboard. The point risked a glance over her shoulder, she saw him silhouetted in the alien green glow of the terminal, its light washing over his face as numbers and symbols scrolled continuously down the screen. She returned her attention to the doors at either end of the hallway, nervously fingering the safety on her weapon. She lifted the muzzle and trained it on the door to her left, then after a moment she switched to the right. After two more shifts, she glanced back again.

"Hurry up," she hissed, "we can't stay here all—" The hallway erupted in explosive noise. The concrete block next to the point's head shattered as a burst of bullets struck it. She spun to see the end of the hallway to her left filling with Judicial guards. The two in the first rank were on one knee and the others were crowding behind them, vying for a shot. She swung her weapon in line with the first shape she saw and squeezed the trigger twice, a fast double-tap. She saw and heard her shots collide with the guard and she ducked into the room. "Shit!" she screamed. "We're blown!" She popped her head back into the hallway and fired two more shots. Two more guards fell. She looked back to see Sigil spin out of the seat and charge in her direction, unslinging his weapon in a smooth, practiced movement. In a moment, she felt his back pressed against hers as his rifle spat at the guards to her rear. The hallway filled with smoke and noise as the initial exchange ran down. To the point, it felt like the moments stretched into hours as she struggled to bring her weapon to bear on the enemy. She felt the sensation of hauling the heavy thing through a sticky fog as everything moved much too slowly. Her arms moved too slowly, her head moved too slowly, Sigil fired too slowly. She couldn't hear or think and the enemy was moving quickly and she was sure that she was going to die.

In the strange, eerie theatre of smoke and heat and chaos, she watched herself from another place and time as she continued to fire and continued to make hits. She saw Sigil through tunneled vision as he reached around her and threw a grenade toward the Judicials on her side and shoved her into the server room. There was a tremendous shock-wave that pushed her from behind and a terrible noise. For a moment, she thought that it was simply that Sigil was in-credibly strong. But it couldn't be. Then she remembered her weapon banging against her head and her weapon sling chafing and burning against her neck as Sigil picked her up and threw her over his shoulder. The top of his shoulder pressed into her gut and she couldn't breathe and then it went black.

SIGIL SQUATTED in the underbrush and meticulously inspected his pack. He patiently went through each piece of gear and laid it on the ground in front of him. He glanced up and saw that the point was slowly rising into consciousness. She brought her hands to her face before she opened her eyes and balled her fists into her eye sockets. She looked past her hands and saw him watching her.

"How did we get here?" she asked sluggishly. Her mouth felt like it was filled with cotton and her head and ears ached with a painful ringing. She winced as the sunlight mercilessly struck her eyes. "Ouch," she said as she lay back and closed her eyes.

"We were successful," said Sigil. "I was able to steal and transmit the code to the satellite before we were discovered. Mission accomplished." His eyes were back in his pack as he rummaged at the very bottom.

"That's not what I asked," she said, "I don't remember anything after you threw that grenade. I was sure we were stuck in there." She twisted her head, looking at him through half-closed eyes. "How did we get here?" she repeated.

He spoke without looking up from the equipment that was laid out before him, "There were too many of them, and the technique that I would have used to leave the building myself could not be utilized by both of us, so I used an entirely different method. You wouldn't understand." He finished with an air of finality that was not lost on the point. "You will be glad to know that we are now the proud owners of a Judicial logistics and communication satellite."

He began to stuff the equipment back into his pack in the reverse order in which it had been removed. "Will you be ready to move soon? This position is too close to the objective. It's not safe." He finished stuffing and securing his pack and shoved hers in her direction. "I repacked your gear while you were out, I hope you don't mind. I felt that we would be in a hurry when you woke up."

She shook her head. "No, I don't mind. Thanks."

"I should be thanking you," returned Sigil. "If you hadn't stayed behind, I don't think I would have cracked that system. It was those last few seconds that counted. You bought me just enough time to finish the job." He paused to let it sink in. "This op would have been totally shot if it wasn't for you. Thank you." He stood, walked the distance to where she lay and extended his hand to her. "We really do have to move though," he said. She shaded her eyes with one hand while grasping his hand with the other. He lifted her easily to her feet but she wobbled dizzily and leaned on his shoulder.

"Where's my weapon?" she asked. "And where are we going?" He handed her the carbine that was slung over his shoulder alongside his own rifle and held her until she was steady.

Looking into the distance at the line of trees that crowned the hilltop, he said, "We're going back to the Abbey. There are some children that I would like you to meet."

SIGIL AND THE POINT crouched atop a building and surveyed the city as it burned. He focused his binos and aimed
them through the smoky haze at the Abbey. He saw the long
supply train and entrenchments of the Judicial lines and he
knew that time was short. He glanced back at the point and
saw that she was watching the Judicial advance as well. "Do
you have family inside the city?" he asked.

She shook her head. "No. I really don't have much of
a reason to be here, I guess. I just didn't feel right about
leaving you in that Sat factory." She grimaced at the scene
below in disgust. "Such a waste."

"Trust me on this," Sigil said, "we both have good rea-
sons to be here and they are inside that chapel." He pointed
to the white building in the distance, its sharp steeple rising amidst the neighboring buildings. "If you felt bad about
abandoning me, then you'll want to help me get those children out of there. It is more important than you could possibly imagine." His face was somber.

She laughed. "You don't have to try and sell me on this,
sir. I hate these Judicial bastards, always have, and I don't
like anyone who targets children. So count me in."

Sigil nodded his thanks and began to descend the fire
escape that had been their means of ascent. The point followed and together they began to carefully make their way
across the rubble-strewn remnants of a once fine city.

THEY FOUND THEMSELVES trapped in one of the last two vaults in the tunnels beneath the Abbey. A large group of Judicial Gunners was setting up a mobile gun battery that aimed down the tunnel and blocked any chance they had of approaching the Abbey. The noise and dust were rolled together into a murky cacophony. The sporadic rattle of gunfire echoed throughout the tunnels and cut through the din of drilling machines.

The point halted and bent to catch her breath and squinted through the clouds of debris. "What's the plan, sir? I think we have about four hundred meters till we hit the Abbey. It doesn't look like there's a way through." She wiped her eyes with the back of her hand and looked at Sigil to see if he was listening. He was in the vault behind her and was digging into the various containers that were stored in the corners of the room. Her curiosity aroused, she backed into the room and pushed the heavy door with her boot. Leaving the vault door cracked slightly, she turned to watch. "What's up, sir?" she asked.

He stopped in the act of tossing various loose articles aside and looked up at her. "There seems to be no reason not to tell you now," he said. "These vaults here beneath the Abbey, they hold archives of data, stored against the day the city fell to the Judicials. We have to get to the children and pull them out of there. We also have to destroy some of these before we leave." He went back to searching through the containers.

"Destroy them?" she asked, "Why? I mean, why go to the trouble to build them if they were only going to be destroyed anyway?" She shook her head at yet another example of administrative stupidity. "Higher ups never make any sense to me," she said. "And just how do you expect to get past that team of Gunners?" she asked doubtfully.

"The reason that I had to gain access to that satellite was because these underground archives have been compromised. The Judicials have located and taken some of them already. I was sent to the satellite facility to hijack a satellite and upload the most important of the archives to the onboard database. All of the data was successfully uploaded yesterday, as you saw. The rest..." he gestured at the room, "cannot end up in Judicial hands." His face showed frustration as he scanned his surroundings. "Don't worry. I'll get past the Gunners. But there should be some sort of initiator or detonator somewhere inside all of these vaults. We may have trouble if we have to pop all of these manually." He paused as he considered the options. Then he looked up at her. "How much training do you have in demolitions?"

MARA WAS AWAKENED by a light that seeped in through the small crack at the bottom of her door. There were noises outside in the passageway and she heard the voices of the few monks that remained in the chapel. She heard the men that had lived in nearly complete silence since she had been brought to the Abbey raising their voices in alarm. She threw back her blanket and hurried to the door. Pressing her ear to the rough wood, she felt shimmering heat and vibration and pulled away in surprise. She focused her ears to the outside and listened. She heard the door to Solomon's room open and she felt him brazenly walk into the hallway. She knew that he was acting more bravely than he truly felt and that he was doing so for her benefit. He never wanted her to see that he was sometimes frightened even though they both knew that she could always tell when he was. The voices of the monks that had filtered up from the bottom floor of the chapel faded abruptly and there was no noise on their level except for Solomon's quiet breath. Mara stood in uneasy suspense and felt an impending doom. Her normal placid and calm smile was absent and she wrinkled her forehead in anxious concern. The light and heat that had silently disturbed her sleep grew in intensity in the hallway. She ventured to split the doorway's jamb and, through the tiny crack that was opened, she saw her brother standing centered in the hallway, facing a man she had never seen. The man saw the crack widen and he looked up and fixed his gaze on the child who was peeking through it. She gasped in amazement and fear as she saw the familiar eyes of her older brother on the face of the stranger. The man set his lips into a grim expression and looked back to Solomon. The boy looked as though he might bolt but he stood his ground.

Finally, the man spoke. "Do you know who I am, boy?" he rasped. Solomon stood frozen in the hall, unable to speak or even move. Mara could sense that he was more frightened than he had ever been. The man spoke again. "Do you have any memories of me?" Slowly, Solomon nodded and the man smiled approvingly. "Yes, Solomon. It has been a long time since I have seen you. I am your father, Thomas Worth."

Mara heard what the man said and she understood the words, but there was no ring of truth to them. She knew that the stranger wasn't lying, but knew even more deeply that what the man said was even worse than a lie. It was something that was true and yet simply wrong. For the first time in her young life, she saw before her something that was unnatural. Not strange or bizarre or weird, but something that was against nature, a fact that was true but, in its very essence, should not have been. She was horrified by the strange man in the hallway and wanted her brother to run from him, but she was too frightened to move or react. She desperately wanted her teddy bear, but he was in her bed next to her pillow and she watched through tearing eyes as the man reached out for Solomon's shoulder. He rested his hand on the boy's arm and squeezed. "Good. I see that you've grown strong in this den of thieves. At least they have made you into something. Now, fetch me your sister."

At the mention of Mara, Solomon pulled away from his father's grasp and glared at him. "What do you care? You don't even know what she looks li—" he started, but before he could finish, Thomas struck him hard across his face.

"Do not raise your voice to me, boy! I am your father and sit in royal privilege. You will soon learn the manners that these fools have neglected to teach you. I tell you again, fetch me your sister or I shall have to fetch her myself." He gripped the boy by his collar and spun him to face Mara's door. "Now, go. Remember who you are." Solomon had a look of illness on his face as he began to slowly walk toward the room. He saw the frightened eyes of his sister, watching him as he approached. The urge that drew him to the room was the same pulling that had tugged at him as he had followed Sigil down the road toward the gray house in the woods, only then it had filled him with energy and now, he felt as if his life was being sucked from him. Mara saw him closing the distance to her door and fled to her bed to snatch up Brownie. Holding her bear before her, she turned to face the door as it opened. The man stood over and behind Solomon as the door swung wide, and she saw the same familiar bitterness in her father's eyes that she often had seen in her brother's. That look was there now but as she knotted her fingers into Brownie's fur, she became calm and smiled. The heat that was entering the room from outside was diminished by the heat that the little girl began to emit. She began to give off a pale, bluish glow and the stones in the wall behind her began to crack and shake. Solomon was taken aback and tried to turn away, but Thomas held him in check.

"Do not yield, boy! She cannot be that strong." Thomas spoke with authority, but the light and heat that came from Mara was more than he or Solomon could bear. When the intensity became so much that they both had to shield their eyes, they turned and ducked their heads into the hallway. The door began to char and smoke and the stones surrounding it started to give way and crumble onto the floor. After a moment the door crashed down into the hall and a cloud of limestone dust rose into the stale, stuffy, overheated air.

When they turned back into the room, Mara was gone. Thomas turned away from the smoldering remains of the door and saw Sigil standing before him, centered in the smoke-filled hall. Sigil knew without thinking that Mara had vanished and that she would be secreted in the stairwell behind him. Since she had read the poem that she had found above the painting, she had taken to spending time in solitude there and it had become a favorite hideout in recent days. He was hopeful that she was unharmed but he had arrived to find Thomas and Solomon standing next to the shattered door.

Thomas peered through the haze and addressed the hooded traveler. "So, I see that you have been the guardian of my progeny, Sitri. Or are you called something else these days, now that you play the role of paladin?" He rested his hand on Solomon's shoulder and the boy felt the strong pressure pressing him into the stone floor. His father's hand felt heavy, like lead, and the pressure was felt inside of his heart as well as on his shoulder. "My children have become strong in your care, Sitri." He guided Solomon to a position behind him and squared himself to Sigil. Sigil responded by arranging himself in a posture of calm stillness, his motion nearly undetectable. Thomas laughed, "Ahh... The tricks and illusions that you learned in the east. I'm afraid that they won't be enough for me. Although I am not as strong as I once was, I too learned a few things in the east."

Solomon wondered where his sister had gone, he had seen her vanish and reappear before but never for very long. She knew that she was not to leave the grounds of the Abbey and so she had only used the power in play. She had been gone for quite a while this time and Solomon began to search through the dust and smoke filled air of the hallway for any sign of her. He sought after her with his mind's eye as he had been taught but to no avail. Panic began to rise inside of him to compete with the tightening dread that was already there. His father stepped toward Sigil and left him standing alone behind him.

He looked up and saw his father forming his hands into a strange and unfamiliar position. With no warning, a charge of energy spread from his father's hands and shot through the dust toward Sigil. A low rumble shook the entire foundation of the chapel as Sigil took the brunt of the shock in his outstretched hands. Solomon had not even seen Sigil move, one moment he had been standing in a position of humble complacency and suddenly, with blinding speed, he had countered the blast that had been directed at him. Solomon pressed himself against the wall and tried to edge past his father. He focused on the stairwell at the end of the passage. His father rose up as though he stood on a cushion of air and simply stepped above the surge of heat and light that had erupted from Sigil's hands.

His father settled gently back to the stones and chuckled. "That was quite impressive, Sitri. When last we met you had no magic at all. You were simply an uneducated soldier. A pawn in The Army of the Lord. And a traitorous one at that. I see that you have picked up a thing or two along the way." His eyes narrowed and his tone changed to ice. "But I have no time for this. Give me the girl. I see in your eyes that you know where she is; even now she hides from me. If she is not given to me, there will be horror that even a Judas like you could never imagine."

Sigil looked at the other man stoically, he ignored the taunt and addressed Solomon. "Do not tell this man a thing, Solomon. The life of your sister depends upon it. As I told you before, he means to kill her."

Solomon stopped in his advance to the stairwell. If he went any further, he realized, his father would see where Mara hid. He looked up at Sigil and then his eyes shifted to his father. He thought of the things that Sigil had told him and of his training with Father Dante. He thought of how easily the magic had flowed through Mara and how hard earned it had been for him. Rage and jealousy rose inside of him. Almost with no thought, his hand slowly began to rise and point to the stairwell.

A grim smile cracked on the face of Thomas Worth. He nodded at his son. "Good child, you have a soul like your father. Strong and fierce. Do not let these weaklings tell you otherwise. She is in the stairwell?" Sigil looked at the boy but did not let his emotions show. He would not scorn the child because he had not been surprised. He also knew that, at one time, he had been a betrayer as well. He slowly closed his eyes and began to mouth the words to the ancient Celestial song. In the stairwell, hiding timidly beneath the cracking masonry, Mara heard and began to softly sing with him. Thomas reached behind him and twisted his hand into Solomon's shirt and ran toward Sigil, dragging the boy in tow. Sigil focused all of his will into one great heave and just as Thomas was upon him, he punched a massive force down into the rocks and cement of the floor beneath him. Behind him, Mara erupted into a brilliant, white light that shone blindingly into the face of Thomas and Solomon. The walls and supports of the chapel caved and crumbled into the tunnels beneath them, carrying Thomas, Sigil and both children down into a roaring chaos. The noise was tremendous, the shock and vibration resounded throughout the surrounding streets. It was heard over the sound of the shells and gunfire of the advancing troops. After a time, it was over. The last pops and cracks of rifles could be heard high above, and Mara lifted her head up into the settling dust. Lying next to her was Sigil, but of her father and her brother, there was no trace at all.

THE POINT FELT an almost physical pressure, the fire from the Judicial gun team was like a blanket that threatened to settle over her and seal her under the earth. She pressed herself to the concrete floor of the vault and prayed sincerely. When she lifted her head, she saw an unearthly scene. She saw Sigil lying unconscious in the tunnel ahead of her and next to him, she saw a small, dark-haired girl. The girl had in her hand a stuffed teddy bear and she was between Sigil and the Gunners. Before the point could react and make any move to warn the child or to save her, the girl raised her empty right hand and made a sweeping motion, a happy smile on her face. The Gunners that stood before her were picked up in a wave of force. The point felt it as a pressure in her ears and eyes and stomach. There was a sensation of crushing weight that was being held back by something unseen, a feeling of a great object held just above her body. The little girl turned her head and smiled a flashing smile at her and held up her teddy bear to make it wave. The point, stunned, waved and smiled a forced smile back at her. Then, the child finished her gesture with her empty hand and the gun team ceased to exist. The point gasped, shocked. One moment the Gunners, their drilling equipment, and their heavy weapons were hanging suspended in the stale, dusty air of the tunnel and in the next instant they were gone, swept away by the little girl's hand.

As the dust began to settle, the point saw a glowing cloud of tiny living beings creating a halo around the girl's hair. They hovered and darted, creating flashes like fireflies against the cracked brick walls of the tunnel. The point heard a noise, just below the ringing in her ears and, as her head cleared of the pressure, she realized that it was music. The little girl was singing softly to herself as the flying creatures hummed an otherworldly accompaniment. The point couldn't make out the words or even be sure that there *were* words but she could see the child's lips moving as she bent over at the waist to look more closely at Sigil's prone form. The stuffed bear nearly touched the tunnel floor and dragged through the dust but the girl noticed and stopped to rearrange her grip so that the bear was safe. She was almost comical to the point as her forehead wrinkled in concern for both the bear and for Sigil; the scene was surreal enough to rouse the point to action.

She stood and hurried over to where the girl was standing. She pretended not to notice the little flying creatures, but inwardly she saw that they were humanoid, and female. She thought to herself *'First things first, get him up and moving and then sort out the hallucinations and shock.'* She was certain that she was experiencing some sort of combat stress related shock. She had seen others that had seen less action than she had react in a far more drastic way and she knew that she wasn't exempt from paying the toll eventually. *'You're fine'* she thought to herself. *'He's in worse shape, so just focus on him right now.'* The little girl stepped backwards, letting the point kneel beside Sigil but she continued to sing the strange, wordless song to herself and to hold out her hand to the creatures, allowing them to alight on her fingers. They sat and watched as the point stripped off Sigil's rifle and harness.

The first explosions rocked the underground chambers with thundering force. Smoke billowed into the tunnels and filled the vault with a gunpowder smell. The point dragged Sigil by his harness, the heels of his boots digging furrows into the collected dust that had gathered on the floor. With the child's help, she pulled him into the first vault that he had shown her, the one with the archives of data and arranged him and his equipment on the floor in the corner. She hoped that the vault would be secure and she listened and kept count of the explosions as they occurred. She had placed three separate charges and Sigil had placed four. She had already counted five as they went off behind them. As she sat back on the floor and rolled her eyes to the ceiling, she gasped and wheezed in an attempt to catch her breath. Another explosion boomed throughout the tunnels and then, nothing.

Silence crowded behind the lingering echoes of the last charge. After they faded, there was nothing. No seventh shot. The point waited breathlessly. She calmed herself and cocked an ear. Nothing. Had she miscounted? She glanced quickly at the child in alarm, "Did you hear another shot go off?" The girl looked at her questioningly. "Another big noise? Ka-boom? How many ka-booms were there?"

The girl held up all the fingers on her empty left hand and one finger on the hand that held her bear. "Six," she replied, "Like how old I am."

The point's forehead wrinkled in dismay. "Six? Are you sure? Only six?" The girl nodded and the point knew that she was right. She thought quickly and realized almost instantly that there was no time. She stood and walked briskly to the door of the vault. "Stay here and watch him, I'll be right back," she said. She opened the vault and walked out into the soot and dust filled tunnel. As she retraced her steps through the passageway, she never saw the small, dark-haired child that followed behind her.

SIGIL CAME to consciousness as a loud shockwave rang in the tunnels. He knew that it was one of the charges that they had laid. He shook his head, as if to clear the dust and debris from his thoughts, then looked quickly around the room to find it empty. A deep, sinking feeling settled into his gut. He pushed back on the floor with his elbows and brought himself slowly to his feet. As he did so, he saw a shock of dark hair flash from the edge of the opened vault door. The hair was followed by a face and a smile and then the rest of Mara. He breathed a deep sigh of relief and wrapped her with an embrace. "Where is the point?" he asked.

Mara's liquid eyes rose up to meet his. "She got lost in the smoke and the noise. I tried to get her but it was too hot. She got lost." Sigil saw the expression in the child's face and knew that Mara was being gentle with him, that the child was being merciful to him and his heart fell. He knew that the point was gone.

Mara looked away from him, to the corner of the room and spoke softly. "It was Corrina," she said, "The girl from the painting and the poem. She pulled you in here." Sigil stood frozen as if he had been struck by lighting. The child wrapped her hands into the fur of her tattered bear and went on, looking away as though she were embarrassed by what she said. "I didn't know if you knew her. She knew you the whole time. *I* knew her as soon as I saw her."

Mara seemed to be aware and conscious of the fact that she saw what others could not and she felt Sigil's pain and confusion. She spoke to him in the same voice that she reserved for Brownie if he was sad. "She missed you and wanted me to tell you who she was. She was sorry that you couldn't see." She sighed and kicked her boot at the rubble at her feet. "You'll find her. Sometime."

She began to look about the vault with the curiosity of a six-year old. She sucked in her breath with excitement, her eyes widening when she saw a trap door in the floor of the vault. Sigil sat on the floor and took in what he had just heard. He kicked shut the door of the vault and pounded his fist into the ground at his side. After a moment, he stood and walked to where Mara was examining the hatch in the floor. He looked back toward the closed door of the vault and heard the noises that were rising on the other side of it. He reached down and held his hand out to the dark-haired girl that stood at his side. Mara looked up at him and smiled her wide, mysterious smile, her hand wrapped around the paw of her bear. She shyly put her other hand in his and looked at him expectantly. The sounds beyond the vault door grew louder. Sigil reached down to the trap door in the floor of the vault and hauled on the handle, opening it. Then, together, he and Mara disappeared into the tunnel below.

Chapter 16

Graphite

If I could but touch the drama and flow of her sketches,
faintly gothic yet solid.
The poetic cartoon shape of each face that she draws
pulls me deeper into her dream.
She wants so badly to be in black and white and only
known by the sadness that she evokes,
but if she rested already in history,
she would never need to prove her worth.
Her pencil traces graphite along the lines of her childhood
and she conjures new worlds filled with graphic heroines.
Of all the novels and stories and films of this world,
hers is a singular shining thread.
Stretching from picture to picture, her work is a faerie opera,
resplendent with whimsy, pathos and charm,
and gorgeous tales and glittering fables reside
within the frame of each vision she creates.
Form and emotion, memory and fantasy seem to collide
gently in the color and shadows of her lines
and I always wished that I could have been born There and not
here.
For perhaps then, I could have caught her eye.

The Fourth Tale

Onlyness

Chapter 17

Anomalie

---

*Of the origins of Anomalie Harper
and the results of The Culture War*

2181 J.D.(Judicial Date) - Judicial Grid 4649

ANOMALIE HARPER let just a sliver of light sneak past her eyelids, just enough to make sure that she was as late as she felt. She lay still beneath her rough blanket and listened to the sound of the city awakening around her. She was definitely late. Her younger brother had left nearly an hour ago and she still hadn't developed even the tiniest inclination to move. How was he able to force himself to go every day? And *on time* every single day. Sometimes he was even early, and Anomalie had never been early for school once. She had been absent almost twenty times this year and late almost all the times she managed to make it. She had been on time once, but *early?* Too much to ask. She buried her face in the single, thin pillow and tried to think of something else. Outside, a trash transport slammed its loader into the wall beneath her window and she winced, dreading the inevitable daily ritual.

"Nomaleee! Wake up! Come to the window!" Wrapping the pillow around her head, she asked herself her morning question, '*Why* was all of this happening to *her?'*

"Nomalee!" The banging loader and the irritating voice drove her out from under her blanket and straight to the window.

"Step back, Justin. Back up off my house. My father doesn't want you anywhere near here." She squinted up through the diffusion of the torn, plastic shade and blocked the rising sun from her eyes with her hand. "Colleen won't like it either." Looking down at the idling trash transport and beyond it to the street she had grown up on, she saw the local riff-raff winding themselves up for another tiring day. Today was no good; there was no way school was happening today. Not for her anyway.

"Colleen doesn't even know I still got this route. She's in school by now anyhow. Or the hospital. Let me come up. C'mon." Justin held his filthy glove to his forehead, shading his eyes in a vulgar salute. He craned his neck to get a better look at the window above him. He watched as Anomalie tucked her head back into her room, a disgusted look on her face. She could barely tolerate Justin when he was with Colleen; his prowling around behind her back was more than she could stand. Slamming shut the window behind her, she ignored the cat-calls that wafted up along with the odor from the trash transport and rummaged through the clothes strewn across her bed. Now that the decision to blow off school had been firmly established, the rest of the day seemed almost bearable. Things never seemed so bad when she spent the day by herself. The only exception to that rule was when she was with Colleen, and even Colleen had a particular habit of driving her up a wall if she was taken in large doses. A little bit of Colleen's insanity went a long way as far as Anomalie was concerned, 'cause she felt that there was enough of that sort of nonsense stuffed inside her own skull. Plus, Colleen spent most of her time with Justin these days and Anomalie was starting to get queasy about that whole train-wreck.

She selected an outfit from the rumpled pile on her bed and held it up in front of her with both hands. Shoving all thoughts of the outside world out of her head, she focused on the reflection in her bedroom mirror. She was too skinny, and her knees were too bony. An ugly, purple bruise went across one shin, growing yellowish near her ankle. She hated her legs anyway so she settled on baggy trousers with enormous cargo pockets that shimmered with an out of date holographic camouflage pattern.

"All the better to not be seen with, my dear…" she whispered to herself, stepping into the pants and twisting her hips to see. She cinched the trousers tight, ignored the surplus material bunched around her waist and moved on to the next item. She held up a black tee, very small, very tight, and looked in the mirror. The logo software was malfunctioning, displaying a series of out of date adverts, flickering between ads for hydration litigators and nanogenetic implants. For a moment, she thought about hacking the shirt and updating the ads, then she thought better of it. "No fashion police where you're going, Lee-Lee. You just have to have it on; you don't have to be current. There's no law about that…" She pulled the shirt over her head and briefly watched the view. "I remember that one…" she murmured to herself. She blinked and squatted to find her shoes. Groping under the bed, she located one, then the other. Vintage Chuck Taylors, the only shoes she would wear anymore. She had lucked out and found a pair on one of her sporadic foraging trips to the Old Zone. Against all odds, they had fit on the first try and right then and there Anomalie had developed faith. The Chucks were probably over a hundred years old and still intact, and they were one of her most valuable possessions. She pulled them on and let the laces hang a little, then sat back on the bed and began to arrange her hair. She separated her blonde hair into two high ponytails with a third, longer ponytail in the back, and tied them all firmly into place. When she was finished, she stood, cocked her head, and looked thoughtfully at her work. The girl who stared critically back at her was a small, athletic sixteen year old, her intelligent green eyes quickly appraising the final effect. Although she was compact, she was well formed, giving the impression of a spring-wound toy, with a sort of hidden, coiled-up energy inside of her. Intricately patterned tattoos were etched on her upper arms and a thin choker of ink made a cat's collar around her neck. Gently almond-shaped eyes, set above delicately sculptured cheekbones, creating a picture infinitely more appealing to the opposite sex than Anomalie would ever have believed possible, completed the feline motif. Anomalie's critique was of a short, skinny, Neo-punk girl who was freakishly tomboyish and who knew that any boy crazy enough to talk to her was way too crazy to trust. After one last twist of her hips, she reluctantly granted her approval and turned about to leave. Almost as an afterthought, she looked back at the mirror, closed her eyes, breathed deeply and intoned softly, "Nobody's a nobody." With that she walked out to the street.

The early morning chill was just starting to burn off as the sun began to warm the concrete. Anomalie let the heavy steel door slam and lock behind her and set off at a quick pace, making a sincere attempt to look past the dismal squalor of her surroundings. Discarded possessions and equally discarded people of all sorts were slowly filling the street, filtering onto the pavement from wherever they'd been hidden during the night. In the periphery of her awareness, Anomalie knew that they were still human. Perhaps only superficially and maybe not completely, but human nonetheless. She felt a distant kinship to the wrecked and ruined neighborhood but, at the same time, she tried to smother any empathy that arose in her. A cynical, aloof tolerance was all she was able to manage. Neatly sidestepping a trio of pre-school aged holos from a daycare ad as they sped toward a group of actual children, she turned the corner and nearly collided with a swinging trash container.

"Hey, oops! Sorry Lee-Lee, almost got ya' with that one. Don't want this stuff all over that pretty blonde hair." She ducked under the container as Justin emptied its contents into the belly of the transport and wove between the other two trashies as they emptied their cans.

"Don't call me Lee-Lee, Justin. It's not my name," she replied curtly, continuing down the sidewalk as Justin tossed his container aside and hurried to catch up.

He fell into step beside her. "But that's what Colleen calls you, she never calls you by your full name. Anyway, I like the way Lee-Lee sounds. It's cute. Like you."

Anomalie caught the clumsy, flirtatious tone in Justin's voice and felt a knot growing in her stomach. Exasperated, she shot back, "You are not Colleen, Justin. And I don't really care what you like. Stop following me." Anomalie started a one-sided conversation in her head. *'What in the world could Colleen see in this idiot? Why did she always have to live in such pain?'* She increased her pace.

"I'm not following you, Lee-Lee, it's a free country. And where are you going anyway? Your school is back that way." It was the last straw. Furious, her eyes flashing, she stopped short.

Turning toward Justin, she blurted out, "Stop calling me that! You know what? It's *not* a free country. You know what else? It's none of your business where I'm going. You may have Colleen snowballed, but I think you're a sucker. Wherever I end up today, I won't be drooling at some school workstation terminal. I won't be in a suicide prevent holo for the third time like Colleen. I won't be dumping trash at zero six. And do you really want to know what, Justin? I wish Colleen had never met you, 'cause there is something really poisonous about your whole vibe." She stood trembling, her feet planted firmly apart and her fists balled tightly. She knew Justin had a reputation for violence, and so she swallowed her fear, showing much more courage than she actually felt. She felt the familiar feeling of turning away from a vicious, unchained dog. Justin's eyes narrowed to dark slits, he looked Anomalie up and down as if to weigh his options. A long moment hung silently in the air between them.

Justin broke first, a wicked sneer forming on his lips. "Yeah. Fine…I know where you're going, Anomalie." He pronounced her name properly, with an exaggerated sarcasm. "Colleen told me all about your little trips to the Old Zone. And people think that *I'm* a criminal. Both of you are nothing but ugly, Neo-punk trash, with out-dated 'plants and uplinks. That's why you both have mental problems, 'cause your circuitry's shot. I hope you get caught in the Zone, Anomalie; they'll lock you up for good this time. And I hope your little, ugly, freak buddy finally figures out how to off herself. I'll be better off without her." He jerked his arm as if to strike her, but Anomalie was already gone, running toward the Old Zone, tears burning in her eyes.

She wandered the vacant streets, killing time as she drifted toward the Zone, waiting for the watch shift to end. The Old Zone was restricted, only representatives of the Judicial Monarchy could freely gain entry, but since most inhabitants of the city had no interest in the Zone, the Judicial still employed human guards. Anomalie had even heard rumors to the effect that the restriction extended to some members of the Monarchy, but as she had no way of confirming those rumors, she treated them as idle gossip. She personally knew of only one other person who had ever been inside the Old Zone, and that was Colleen. She herself had been sneaking in since she was ten years old, and she had never seen another living soul inside the fenceline. The watchmen who patrolled its outskirts were Judicial Legionnaires, as battle-hardened as any, but they viewed their post as a formality, owing to the fact that no one in their right mind would actually *want* to enter the Old Zone. Bizarre electrical effects, random static storms that could play havoc with your implants, ghostlike holographic avatars of long-dead unwired humans, these were just a few of the hazards of the Zone. Relics of a happily forgotten past, phantoms from before the Culture War. In the eyes of the average legionnaire, the Monarchy should simply issue the order to nuke the place and be done with it. This forbidden and forbidding sector of a city renowned for its harshness, bleak and solitary behind razor-wire fences, this had become Anomalie's playground.

She paused and checked her chrono and saw that she would have to hurry to catch the next shift change. *'Lousy, stinking display...'* she thought to herself as she checked the time and her location. Most people could prompt and view their heads-up display, or HUD, while they were walking, the current holos were fourth or even fifth gen, but Anomalie's cranial implant was a rewired second-generation system. The holo wasn't quite transparent and she tended to stumble if she read and walked at the same time. *'One day I'll be rich and I won't depend on this jacked up gear...'* She saw that her window to enter the Zone would be closing soon so she deactivated her HUD and anxiously hurried on. There was only one shift change available to her on a school day if she had any intention of making it home before her father.

She had refined her methods of entering the Zone through countless experiments; a few times she had been caught and, once, detained. She shuddered at the memory of her detention and reminded herself of her vow to never be caught again. She approached the fenceline slowly, keeping well out of sight of the nearest guardhouse. Several of the legionnaires could probably recognize her by sight, but none had been on duty the last time she'd been caught, and they didn't regard a skinny, teen-aged, loitering female as a serious threat. She took a vague, meandering route that wound through alleys and walkways toward a crumbling building that overlooked the guardhouse. Along the way, she passed the outgoing guard detail and waved shyly at the commanding legionnaire. He reacted to her gesture as though an especially unpleasant odor had blown through his respirator, but the junior conscript who was in the rear of the party nodded almost imperceptibly. She acknowledged his response by batting her eyelashes obligingly and staring stupidly at her sneakers. She maintained the position that if she *was* ever caught and detained again, any friend at all might help. As the legionnaires passed, she rolled her eyes and, casting an amused glance at the retreating back of the conscript, chuckled inwardly, *'In your dreams, you Judi robot.... never in a million years, not with a jacked up Judi clone. Never. Period.'* But Anomalie couldn't get over a nagging sensation that, in spite of herself, she was just a bit flattered. At least one of them had noticed, so she couldn't be that bad. Justin could go to hell, or at least back to wherever he went when he wasn't slinging trash. Mortified that she had shown such weakness, she scurried across the remaining avenue and into the dilapidated building.

Once inside, she let loose a restrained sigh of relief. The newly posted guards could probably have heard her from where they stood, but, at the moment, they were busily shouting and relaying orders to one another. She was hidden from sight by the remnants of a low wall that ran almost perpendicular to, and nearly touched, the fenceline. On her side of the wall was a shallow trench that descended into a tunnel. It had remained undiscovered for so long simply because of its proximity to the guardhouse. Anomalie had discovered it by one of those windfalls of luck that are so unique to children of misfortune. As a small child, ten years old, she had been engaged in the usual employment reserved for youngsters from her neighborhood, that of begging from occupying Judicial Troopers. With a keen and practiced eye, she had spied a satcom-uplink dangling, unsecured from the battle harness of a distracted trooper. Ever vigilant for such opportunities, she had followed him, at a distance, for the remainder of his patrol. The uplink was priceless, because with it, she would be able to upgrade her own terra 'plants to sat 'plants and wouldn't be behind at school. The patrol, with little Anomalie in pursuit, had terminated at the previously mentioned guardhouse and Anomalie, with remarkable patience for one so young, had positioned herself behind the wall. She awoke hours later to find the trooper with the uplink gone, the new shift asleep in the guardhouse, and the tunnel leading into the Old Zone. She knew of other ways in, but she had never been caught at the tunnel. When she was pressed for time, the tunnel was the first way, and still the best.

Now she crept, barely breathing, along the wall toward the mouth of the tunnel. It seemed, to her, that she had always done this, that she couldn't remember a time before the Zone. She was afraid of the legionnaires and of being caught, but she couldn't imagine staying away. At one point, when she was midway along the wall, a legionnaire sat on the ledge directly above her, his harness and weapon settling against her head. As he shifted his weight, she moved silently on, frightened yet stoic and determined. She thought of the countless times that she had been in that exact spot, and the thought gave her confidence. Finally, like a coin in a magician's hand, Anomalie passed under the fenceline and vanished into the Old Zone.

Chapter 18

Flashback

Of Sigil's awakening
and of Anomalie's lair

DEEP WITHIN the labyrinthine mazes of the Old Zone, buried beneath shattered, concrete walls, a computer interface revved awake. Dormant and dust-covered for years, it clicked, then hummed and came to life with a soft glow.

```
:   LABEL QUERY--
TEMPORAL SHIFT PROMPT--
CHECKING RELEVANT PROTOCOLS--
```

Sigil was back in school...the dreams were always about school. They were never about operations or the barracks, certainly never about civilian life or women. It was always school, a never-ending nightmare of training. The platoon stood in a circle around the instructor, at parade rest. The instructor spoke loudly, in an abrupt staccato, gesturing with his hands. Just beyond the instructor, hanging translucent in the air, Sigil could see Angelic script scrolling as if it was in a computer terminal. That wasn't right, it didn't belong there...

"The acronym you will use for your entry format will be CIRCLES. You are expected to take detailed notes. Break out pen and paper. CIRCLES signifies as follows: 'C', clear intent, 'I', intel and insertion, 'R', rehearsals, 'C', communication, 'L', lookouts, 'E', egress, and 'S', sterilize, the most important step. Repeat it." The platoon sounded off,

"C" - CLEAR INTENT!
"I" - INTEL & INSERTION!
"R" - REHEARSALS!
"C" - COMMUNICATION!
"L" - LOOKOUTS!
"E" - EGRESS! And
"S" - STERILIZE! THE MOST IMPORTANT STEP!

ANOMALIE WAS SMILING as she emerged from the tunnel into the shining sunlight. She had the whole day to herself. For an instant, she wished Colleen could have been there so that they could have shared the solitude, but then she recognized the contradiction and shrugged it off. Colleen would never have forgotten the world outside the fence-line; she would have brought her issues inside with her, and that would defeat the whole idea of the Zone. Here, amidst the cracked and decaying foundations of the city, Anomalie was issue free. The pressing weight of her life at home and school seemed to fall away and an eager lightness replaced it. Still cognizant of the guardhouse behind her, she quietly slipped into a conveniently shadowy alley.

A SIGNIFICANT AMOUNT of heat was now radiating from the entombed computer. As if attempting to make up for lost time, circuits unused for decades began firing in a flurry of activity.

```
:   LABEL ARCHIVE--RUNNING
TEMPORAL SHIFT INITIATED--
DIAGNOSTICS INITIATED--
```

The instructor was just one of many, and the classes began to blend seamlessly together. A constant repetition of basic principles had been mercilessly drilled into the platoon. Fire and movement, close combat, raids and ambushes — these were the fundamentals. Covert entry was a master class, a virtuoso performance. The instructor continued, but Sigil continued to see the Angelic script. He glanced furtively at the other recruits on either side of him. They didn't seem to notice. Now, he could see, interspersed with the Angelic symbols, rapid-fire lines of computer code. Assembly language. The instructor droned on,

"C" - CLEAR INTENT

"The intent should state the clear parameters of every phase of the entry, particularly those of the final outcome. Every member of the entry team should understand these parameters. The extent of the footprint allowed should be known. This "allowable footprint" will be dictated by situation.

"The intelligence phase of the entry never ends. The intelligence gathered should be precise to the most minute aspect. Everything, no matter how small, is important. Avenues of approach into and out of the area of operation should be mapped. Adjacent areas must be studied. A mental picture or model of the interior of the structure should be constructed. Lock mechanisms and alarm systems must be studied in detail. Police and civilian activity in the objective and surrounding areas needs to be observed. AT NO TIME should the gathering of intelligence have an effect on the habits of enemy personnel. The habits and routines of personnel on and around the objective are crucial to survey, but a plan must be able to adapt to unexpected changes. Your intelligence scenario must be updated as these changes occur. Intel should develop a variety of options and your planning should reflect this."

ANOMALIE KNEW where she was going, and she took the most direct route. The ambient interference in the alley was causing her HUD to flicker on and off, and the buzzing was beginning to irritate her. Some days were better than others, but on days like this, when the background static was high, it was safer inside. The electromagnetic distortion would occasionally trigger hallucinations or more benign lucid dream states. Anomalie enjoyed the dreams, but the hallucinations terrified her. Squinting carefully at the ground in front of her, she hurried on.

THE COMPUTER BEGAN transmitting. The transmission was a tight-beam tertiary code, piggy-backed onto a modulated laser. Thinner than one one-thousandth of a human hair, the beam erupted from what looked like the skeletal remains of an ancient radio tower, bolted atop one of the only intact structures inside the Zone. The computer itself was inside the structure, or rather beneath it. Rapidly processing the initial data that began to flow from other components of the tower, the computer made adjustments, and swept the beam through the midday sky.

```
:  LABEL RETRIEVAL--
SEARCHING--
UPDATE;
SATELLITE UPLINK--
INITIATED-- STANDING BY TO METALOAD---
```

"Circles?" If you thought about it, it was absurd. 'Why circles?' It seemed like they had a silly acronym for everything, even eating. If you thought about it, you would wonder which genius came up with all of them. But he never thought that hard about it, that was why he was there. He seldom thought anymore, he simply trained. He tried to focus on the class and the instructor's voice, but a nagging sensation was beginning to grow inside him. The Angelic script became clearer, more defined, and the computer code suddenly increased in complexity. The instructor went on,

"I" - INSERTION

"Planning of the insertion phase should begin as soon as information begins to be collected. The sensitive nature of the insertion method should not be overlooked. The egress and insertion should be along different routes. The insertion vehicle (if a vehicle is used) should not be posted as a lookout, nor remain stationary. Alternate methods of insertion (such as foot mobile, trains, etc.) should be examined. Extraction is just as important as insertion. The team should take care not to 'break for the barn' and must follow through on all tactical measures."

SHE WAS HEADING for the Bunkers, a series of enormous cargo bays that were situated near the center of the Zone. Built like fortresses, they had remained standing during the nuclear exchanges that had been common during the early part of the Culture War. The area immediately surrounding them was littered with refuse from some of the most intense fighting of the war, and it was there that Anomalie had scavenged some of her most precious treasures. She was still at least a mile away, and she periodically stopped to check her bearings. Although she had been exploring the Zone for years, she'd learned quickly that the Zone could be deceiving. After one particularly heart-pounding day of being completely disoriented, she swore she would never be lost again. She prompted her HUD and accessed a city-planning map. The map was a tri-d upgrade of an old two-dimensional graphic, so she was supposed to stand still and superimpose it over the local view. No such luck. The sheer volume of radiating energy that was present in the Old Zone, combined with the low-resolution city map, was producing a garbled mess. Lately, her implants had been malfunctioning even under the best conditions. She blinked and shook her head as the heads-up display faded. *'Today is just not your day, Lee-Lee,'* she thought to herself as she surveyed the landmarks around her, *'I guess you'll have to do it up old-school stylee.'* Her ponytails flashed as she swung her head left, then right, her forehead wrinkling. Then, making up her mind, she moved on.

THE BUNKERS were haunted. There were "ghosts" in the machines. The computer was aware of other systems operating in the region, but they were not immediate concerns. It was concerned with only four systems, and only one of those was its primary directive.

```
:   LABEL DIRECTIVE--
INITIATE METALOAD
QUATERNARY DIRECTORY;
TREVOR--LOADING
TERTIARY DIRECTORY;
MEEKO--LOADING
SECONDARY DIRECTORY;
WALTER--LOADING
STANDBY--
RECALIBRATING TO METALOAD
PRIMARY DIRECTIVE--
DETECTING OUT-OF-PHASE MEMORY STREAM--
ADJUSTING--
```

He wasn't always certain that he was still dreaming, 'Was this before the war? Had he enlisted again?' He could read the chunks of Angelic that were visible, but the computer code was illegible to him. The instructor shifted in and out of focus slightly, making it harder to concentrate on the class, and Sigil realized that this was neither a dream nor reality. There was always a chance that he had overlooked something, there was always confusion and doubt. When in doubt, train harder. That was what he had been taught. He shifted his boots in the sand and focused on the instructor.

"R" - REHEARSALS

"Rehearsals will be as realistic as possible. They must be conducted to estimate time lines as well as for practical application. If possible, locks, alarm sensors, even doors and windows of the same type should be procured. Reverse planning should apply so that simultaneous actions occur on the objective. Realism is key as options for tools and techniques will develop through rehearsal. Walk-throughs and talk-throughs should be conducted intermittently. Initial reconnaissance probes can be used as rehearsal 'sketches'. When everything else is done, rehearse again. Plan for the unexpected to happen on the objective and practice with random 'cogs' thrown into the plan."

ANOMALIE HAD A PLACE inside the Bunkers, a place that even Colleen had never seen. Had Colleen been with her, the two of them would have found another place to amuse themselves. This place was different, special. Somehow, in her heart, Anomalie knew that Colleen wouldn't have understood it, that it would have frightened her. For all their similarities, for all their shared memories and experiences, she and Colleen were not alike, and it was because of this place that she knew it. As she neared the Bunkers, she felt it as a sort of massive object, with a gravity that pulled and transformed her. The people who knew her out past the fenceline, the characters from her life, they barely would have recognized her, they would have been shocked. Gone were the bitter, furrowed eyebrows, replaced by an expression of excited anticipation. Her normally combative swagger had become a hopeful, rushing gait. She resembled the child she once had been.

THE COMPUTER sent a series of rapid-fire signals to a device that was hardwired into its system. The device resembled an electrically wired coffin and was effectively concealed inside the catacombs beneath the Bunkers. Casket-like in its exterior appearance, it was actually constructed quite differently and its contents were of a quite different sort. As the current began to flow through the container, the delicately monitored environment within began to slowly change.

```
 :   LABEL CONFIGURED--
GEOSYNC POSITION STABILIZED
INBOUND TELEMETRY STABILIZED--
OUT-OF-PHASE MEMORY STREAM STABILIZING--
LOADING PRIMARY DIRECTIVE
TEMPORAL SHIFT PROMPT CODE VERIFIED--
SENDING CODE......
```

Suddenly he felt wide-awake. He hadn't felt tired before, yet the difference between then and now was pronounced. The foggy, translucence of the Angelic letters came sharply into focus and solidified; the instructor's voice became softer, more distant.

"C" - COMMUNICATION

"The internal communication net within the entry team is essential to the security of the mission. A communication plan should be established that is comprehensive. Call signs for each moving or stationary element should be assigned, as well as alternates and alternate frequencies. Brevity codes for phases of the entry, positions, contingencies and abortion should be established. Verbal communication should be kept to a minimum within realistic parameters. Frequencies and call signs should change AT LEAST once during the operation. One member of the team will be assigned the task of monitoring external transmissions. Adequate time should be spent scanning and locating police patrol, dispatch, alarm dispatch and any other pertinent radio frequencies. This team member will be familiar with radio technique and relevant external codes."

SHE CAME to a ventilation duct that led into the Bunkers, a narrow concrete passage that burrowed down to the catacombs below. Kneeling so that she could enter, she looked uneasily over both shoulders, an inexplicable feeling of being watched settling over her. She hesitated and glanced around her again, a perplexed look on her face. *'Get a grip, Lee-Lee, there's no one out here.'* Frowning, she stood and turned her back on the Bunker, her mind contemplating what it might be and dreading the worst. *'Please, not another hallucination, please not now...'* She flicked on her heads-up and scrolled through the spectrum. She tried infrared, then thermal, and then she finally caught something on her oscilloscope. Something was vibrating above her, on the roof of the building. She backed up. There it was. She saw it now. A tiny, rusty radio-satellite array was moving. *'That's gotta be a glitch,'* she marveled. She covered her temples with her hands, trying to shield her 'plant from the static, and magnified the view. It was definitely moving. She checked the waveform on the scope again just to make sure and she was right, the little tower was humming away up there like it was built only yesterday and hadn't had a million nukes dropped right on top of it a century ago. *'Tough little machine,'* she thought, but she wasn't surprised. Nothing was surprising in the Old Zone; that was why she came here. She turned around, crawled into the duct, and started her descent to the catacombs.

THE COMPUTER had acknowledged that Anomalie had entered the building, and had registered that she had scanned the roof. Busily recording her biological and cybernetic profile, it monitored her progress into the lower levels of the building and continued with its original task.

```
:   LABEL SECURITY--
HUMAN FEMALE; CYBER-ENHANCED--
SYSTEM; NON-SPECIFIC--
UPGRADES; UNKNOWN--
VECTORING--216 METERS; CLOSING
: LABEL DIRECTIVE--
TEMPORAL SHIFT; INTERNAL TEMPERATURE
STABILIZED--
TEMPORAL SHIFT--IMMINENT;
STANDBY.....
```

He felt like he was about to pass out, or rather to pass in. The class, the instructor, the platoon, they were unreal, insubstantial. He was real, he was substantial. They were coming back to him in bits and pieces, fragmented memories and experiences. This wasn't a class from boot camp, it couldn't be. Still, he wasn't sure, he still felt doubt. The Angelic letters scrolled past and he tried to make sense of them, but now the computer code intertwined with them and obscured any meaning. The assembly language began to predominate, crowding out the Angelic.

"L" - LOOKOUTS

"Lookouts are the security element of the entry team. Their role is not to engage or make contact with those who would discover or compromise the team's activities. Their primary task is to serve as an early warning system for the team members operating inside the area of operations. This does not mean that they will not use pretexting to hinder or delay any intruders or patrols. Their goal is to widen the time 'window' within which the team will temporarily halt, and then resume the operation or abort. Placement of lookouts should optimize this time 'window' and provide maximum coverage of avenues of approach and/or observation points.

"An observation point is any position where direct line of sight runs from an entry team member's position to that point. Lookouts will not be stationary unless they can be concealed. By pulling outward from the AO, lookouts can observe multiple avenues of approach and observation points. Lookouts must be proficient in specific skills such as comsec techniques, surveillance/counter surveillance."

SHE POPPED OUT of the ventilation duct and dropped the six feet to the floor of her room. Cluttered from floor to ceiling, the room was a perfect expression of Anomalie Harper. Posters and clippings lined the walls, the floor was carpeted with comics and hand printed fanzines. The result of years of cherry picking through the residue of an irradiated combat-zone, the room was home to her. It was furnished with vintage, pre-Culture War artifacts, lovingly and meticulously restored and decorated with one dominating theme. Music. Punk-rock music. The rescued posters and stickers that covered nearly every square inch of wall space represented hundreds of bands from the last quarter of the twentieth century. Looming in one corner was a giant, archaic sound system, with tangled knots of wires and cables protruding from all sides. On the floor in front of it were crates of records and piles of tapes and CDs. Squatting next to the system, she poked through the tapes until she finally settled on one. Flipping open the scratched case, she removed the tape and read it. "Misfits, perfect..." she spoke aloud to herself, and inserted the tape into the antique tape deck. It whirred with a slight grinding noise and began to rewind the tape. Anomalie drifted a bit while the machine labored. *'That little radio tower sure looked like it was tracking a sat,'* she thought. *'But no Judicial array could look like that.'* There wouldn't be equipment from the Monarchy this far inside the Zone either, she reasoned. Would there? The idea worried her, what if they found this place? Impossible. She pushed the thought from her mind and pressed play on the tape deck. As the Misfits started blasting out "Horror Business", she flopped backwards onto her bed and closed her eyes.

THE TASK that the computer had been designed for was nearly complete. It created one final snapshot file of Anomalie and sent it to the tower, which, in turn, sent it to space. Then, its circuits cooling, its interface dimming, it shut down.

```
:   LABEL ONLINE--
TERRA LINK TERMINATED--
MACDOUGLAS GEOSYNC SUPPORT SYSTEM F505
FULLY OPERATIONAL--
"WELCOME BACK, TEAM--!"
AI CYBERNETIC UNIT TREVOR; OPERATIONAL--
AI CYBERNETIC UNIT WALTER; OPERATIONAL--
AI HOLOGRAPHIC UNIT MEEKO; OPERATIONAL--
"SIGIL, ARE YOU AWAKE?"--
```

He definitely heard that. He looked closely at the instructor, who was still conducting the class.

```
"SIGIL, IF YOU HEAR THIS, DO NOT ATTEMPT
TO RESPOND. YOU ARE EXPERIENCING MEMORY
SHIFT. IT WILL RESOLVE IN APPROXIMATELY
FOUR MINUTES."
```

What the hell was that? A feeling of panic welled up in his chest. He knew that voice, a disembodied ghost from the past.

```
"PLEASE STAY CALM. YOU ARE EXPERIENCING
PRIOR MEMORY STREAMS. THE STREAMS WILL
TERMINATE WHEN YOU REGAIN CONSCIOUSNESS.
PLEASE STAY CALM."
```

He breathed deeply and listened to the class.

"E" - EGRESS

"The egress plan should NOT be the insertion in reverse. The entry team should be able to move into the egress phase at any point after going 'hot'. The team should plan for team withdrawal, element withdrawal and individual withdrawal. Rally points must be used and familiar to team members. Alternates must be developed and rehearsed. At all costs, the entry team must avoid being 'boxed in'. If the team is at risk of this, the abort code will be called. ALL team members must abide the abort code. Undue caution must be avoided, but mission accomplishment is not paramount. Safety is."

THE POUNDING MUSIC usually took her away from worry, but her mind kept returning to the tower on the roof. The Old Zone was filled with unusual and unpredictable oddities, but they were generally effects of the strange electrical fields prevalent in the area. They messed with your hardware and sometimes your software but they weren't real. That tower was *real*, objective, and somebody had put it there. It had been activated and it was tracking something in the sky. What if they were coming back for it? What if they were here in the building? She sat up on the bed with a troubled countenance.

THE HUGE, MACDOUGLAS class geosynchronous satellite, positioned miles above the Old Zone, had received the baton from the tiny computer below. As it came online, it began transmitting directly to the occupant of the coffin-like container that was hidden inside the Bunkers.

```
:   LABEL DIALOGUE--
TRIGGERING AUDIO--
"SIGIL, YOU ARE NOW ALMOST FULLY CONSCIOUS.
THE DISORIENTATION WILL WEAR OFF QUICKLY.
DO NOT BE ALARMED. YOU WILL NEED TO MOVE
IMMEDIATELY. A PARTIALLY CYBERNETIC
OPERATOR, FEMALE, IS DIRECTLY ABOVE
YOUR POSITION.
I'M UNLOCKING THE BOX. PUT IN THE EARPIECE,
PLEASE."
```

Before he had *felt* awake, now he *was* awake. The vision of basic training disappeared as he opened his eyes and saw the inside of a tightly cramped box, illuminated with a faint reddish glow. He groped at his side and felt the earpiece with numb, tingling fingers. He could barely move, but he managed to get the earpiece to his ear. As he did, he felt the reassuring pressure of his rifle next to him. He heard the class in his ear; the instructor's voice was an artificial, static-filled recording.

"S" - STERILIZE

"Sterilization discipline for the entry team is two-fold. Firstly, it consists of sterilizing the team's gear and personnel. Secondly, it consists of a continuous policing of the AO. All tools, equipment and vehicles will be taken down and cleaned for the event of jettisoned gear. While the team is 'hot', constant attention should be given to cleaning while you work. This is to minimize time on target in the event an abort code is called. The AO is never clean enough! The smallest item is enough to generate leads."

ANXIOUSLY, Anomalie turned off the music and listened. There, she heard it again, a mechanical noise from below her. There was a door leading out of her room but she seldom used it. It opened into the main corridors of the building and they were filled with rubble and debris. She knew though, that if she had to get out, they were far faster than the ventilation duct. Terrified, she moved to the door and put her ear against it.

The satellite noted that she had silenced the music and had changed her position. Updating her profile, it passed the data along.

"SHE IS ON THE MOVE, SIGIL. I HAVE NO
COROLLARY DATA. THERE IS A STAIRWAY
DIRECTLY AT THE FOOT OF THE BOX, DO YOU
REMEMBER? SHE APPEARS UNARMED, BUT HER
IMPLANTS ARE NOT IN MY DATABASE. TREAT AS A
HOSTILE."

Sigil remembered the stairway, vaguely. In a daze, he rolled out of the box, grasping his weapon and struggling to keep his balance. He moved to the stairs as rapidly as his condition would allow and quietly slid back the bolt on his weapon. The voice droning in his ear was finishing the class.

"SOFTENING" the AO

"The technique of softening is to simultaneously reconnoiter and disarm or attack specific breach points in the target area perimeter. The team should view the AO security as not only a perimeter but also as entry lanes. This is because it may be possible to disarm or attack some, but not all of the sensors or locking mechanisms in the AO. The system, as a whole, will probably not be defeated. Only one door, window, lock, passive or active sensor may need to be accessed. The entry team should look to exploit human error in the system. It is usually the most consistent. Potential softening techniques include accessing the alarm sensors when the system is disarmed, replacing locks, re-combinating locks, stealing keys and codes, copying keys, accessing the underlying operating system or CPU, false alarming and modifying door mechanisms. Some of these require probes within the perimeter during 'daylight hours'. This list is not exclusive."

PANICKING, Anomalie yanked open the door and bolted down the corridor, memories of the Judicial detention center spurring her on. She couldn't go back there, she wouldn't make it through again. *'Please, let me get out. I swear I'll never come back again. I swear.'* Tears streaming down her face, she knew she was trapped. The Judicials were never alone; if they were below her then they were above and all around her too. Her legs pumping, her chest heaving, she ran in desperation, hoping to make it to the stairway that led to the upper levels. Turning a corner, she saw the stairway and her face brightened. At almost the same instant, a figure rose on the stairs from the level below, and she found herself staring into the barrel of a very deadly looking rifle and two very determined eyes.

Chapter 19

A Calling

*Of Muru's awakening
and of Anomalie's past*

S HE stopped short, a strangled breath catching in her throat. Her body was shaking badly, from a mixture of adrenaline and the electrical discharge that was emitting from her 'plants. They were struggling to keep up with the sudden surge of energy that had just flooded her nervous system. She started to backpedal and the man spoke.

"Stop! Don't move!" he barked, and she froze, confused. He sounded human, like a regular person, not like the enhanced vocal sound that usually came out of a legionnaire's respirator. He looked human too, and sick. She peered timidly at the eyes behind the rifle that was aimed at her and slowly took in the entire scene. Her 'plants were working feverishly to regulate her breathing and, as fresh oxygen was forced into her blood, her gasping slowed. She saw that it wasn't a Judicial Legionnaire that held her at gunpoint; it wasn't anything she recognized at all. It was male, and apparently human, and clearly in need of medical attention. He was shaking at least as much as she was, and was barely able to keep the rifle trained on her.

He adjusted his grip and spoke again. "Who or what are you?" he rasped out. "Identify yourself."

She suddenly noticed the clothes that he was wearing, the vaguely familiar military pattern.

"I-I-I'm Anomalie...Anomalie Harper." she stammered. "Grid four-six-four-niner, school division two-two—"

He cut her off abruptly. "Are you a cyborg?" he asked, leaning against the wall of the stairwell. He looked as if he might faint.

"What?" she returned, not understanding. "What do you mean?" A strange thought was starting to form in her mind.

"Cybernetic. A robot," he snapped and slumped to one knee, his eyes dropping.

"Aren't you?" she replied, and then it dawned on her. The uniform, the rifle, the strange questions. Anomalie's mouth fell open. Incredulous, a look of amazement on her face, she whispered, "Who or what are *you*?" She prompted her heads-up and scanned him, head to boots, switching through the various screens. She held her hands very still as she checked him, 'cause he was still pointing the gun at her. Her display revealed three distinct things about him. Firstly, his vital signs were dangerously weak. Secondly, he was receiving data from and sending data to a satellite, using a device in his ear, and thirdly, he had no implants at all. He was unwired. She was in awe. *Unwired.* She couldn't believe her eyes. With a single fluid motion, she stepped forward and stripped the rifle from his hands, and with a final, struggling effort, he toppled forward, unconscious.

"I always wanted to do that," she muttered, smiling to herself.

SIGIL OPENED HIS EYES to a collage of images plastered above him. He was lying on the bed in Anomalie's room below the Bunkers, the ceiling above him was a sprawl of clippings and photos, taken from hundreds of yellowed magazines and newspapers. He felt weak. His head lolled to one side and he saw her crouching next to a giant stereo.

"Hey…" he attempted feebly, but she couldn't hear him over the music. He tried again, louder this time, "Hey…you, where is my rifle?" She turned her head and gazed at him thoughtfully for a moment, then stood and walked to the side of the bed. She stood above him, studying him, as though he was a newly discovered species placed atop a dissecting table. She extended her arm and pointed to the corner.

"I have it," she said. "It's safe." He groaned as he tried to raise himself to his elbows and gave up, unsuccessful. She knelt and brought her face closer to his, closely inspecting his eyes, a look of wonder in her own. "Who are you?" she whispered. Sigil knew when he was beaten, he was in no condition to resist and the girl obviously meant him no harm. He returned her inspection, noticing the input jacks imbedded in her skin near her ears.

'Should have expected that, Sigil' he thought, and taking a breath, he replied to her question. "I am part of the lead element of a special operations capable unit, responsible for limited, search and destroy missions in this sector." He took another quick breath and finished rapidly, "Your duty as a citizen is to assist me in rejoining my team." He paused, holding his breath, reading her expression. At his side, he crossed his fingers as he waited for her response.

She sat back on her haunches, digesting what she had just heard. Then, quietly at first, but with increasing energy, she started laughing. "No you're not!" she giggled, "Whatever you are, you're no Judicial. I know Judies, and you are definitely not one of them." She stopped laughing and her eyes became serious. "Listen mister, you can tell me. I hate the Judicial Monarchy. I won't tell 'em that you're here. I hide out here myself." She gestured at the disorder around her. "Does this look like a Judicially sanctioned environment?"

He was still unsure of the exact details of how he had gotten there, the memories were still fragmented, but he knew that he was supposed to have been revived by monks of the Order of Dismas, most likely in a monastery of some sort, not by a bionic teenager, in what appeared to be a punker's squat. Something had obviously gone wrong with the instructions he had left in place with the Order, or with the satellite itself. He decided to take a chance. He glanced at her as if appraising her ability to believe and shifted his eyes back to the ceiling.

"You're right…" he began slowly. "Anomalie, right?"

"Call me Lee-Lee," she said.

"Lee-Lee…fine. Look, Lee-Lee, how much do you know about the Culture War?" He looked fleetingly at her and saw her expression change. She looked away. There was an awkward silence.

Finally, she spoke. "Communication about the war is not sanctioned. Data about events leading up to the war is tagged-*restricted*, physical objects that are time-stamped as pre-war are tagged-*restricted*—"

He broke into her monotone recital, "What is all this stuff, then? That tape you're playing is from before *my* time…" He stopped, realizing, too late, that he'd slipped and dated himself. She stood up, turned her back to him and drifted across the room to pick a wrinkled, torn magazine up off of the floor. She held it carefully, and looked wistfully at the cover. The picture was of a woman, holding a microphone, standing on a stage. Behind the woman was a guitarist, both of them frozen in the passionate act of music. Anomalie stared into the picture, saw the sepia faces of the long-dead crowd.

She turned back to face Sigil, her expression hardening. "I know who you are," she said, pointing at his tunic. "I've seen people in uniforms like that before. In one of these!" She held up the magazine. "But you should be dead. You all *died*." She backed away from him as he quickly sat up and swiveled to place his feet on the floor. Still seated, he held up his hand and made a subtle gesture in her direction. She felt a buzzing in her 'plants and then a soothing hum took its place. She slowly lowered herself to the floor.

"I need you to remain calm, Lee-Lee," he said, "I need you to trust me for just a little while longer. I can explain more when I have more of an idea of what's going on my-self." He lay back on the bed and took a risk. "What year is it anyway?" She was aghast. She had seen sci-fis before and she knew what was going on. This freak was playing a role, pretending that he was in some sort of pre-war Terminator vid. She had run into some really hardcore fiction junkies over the years, she had even fallen into it herself for a while. She prepared herself for fight or flight because she knew that they could be unpredictable. Slowly, she started to creep to-ward the air-duct, trying to position herself between the guy and his rifle.

No sooner had she moved than he spoke again. "Stop," he said. "There is no reason for you to run. I just need to know how far we have come."

For some strange reason, the tone that the guy spoke in was impossible not to trust. Anomalie stopped her advance and looked more intently at him. "It's 2181 J.D., same as yesterday," she said.

He lifted himself off of the bed and shook his head to clear it. After a moment of thought he said, "One hundred and sixty-five years..." He walked past her and picked up the rifle. "Come, I have to show you something."

THEY WALKED ABREAST of each other through the passages, back toward the stairway where they had met. Anomalie was not willing to let this decidedly unstable and armed man get behind her. He wasn't about to lose track of her ei-ther. They quickly negotiated the route back to the chamber where Sigil had recently been dormant. The casket-like container remained as he had left it, and he looked purposefully around the room until he found the thing that he sought. In an alcove, behind the container and various pieces of pre-war equipment, he found it. It was a large case, shaped like a footlocker, with a heavy lock on it; Sigil went to it and began to manipulate the lock.

Anomalie watched for a moment and was unable to keep the attitude out of her voice. "Manual analog lock? Physical system? Not very secure, even for pre-war, no?" She assumed a slight smile and a belligerent pose, she was beginning to tire of humoring this guy. Sure, he had a way about him, but she should never have let him get near his rifle. Mistake. She wouldn't beat herself up over it though, she would just make up for it by leaving him behind, first chance she got. She would find another place to stash her stuff.

Suddenly, her eyes grew wide as the man's hands slid through the case and into the floor beneath it. She put her hands up to the side of her face and fired up her HUD. This was a new trick. She wasn't sure if it was a Bunker induced hallucination, or just some new techie effect that she wasn't familiar with yet. It was cool though, she had to give him that. His hands were deep in the concrete now and he appeared to be reaching and searching for something. There, he found it. She saw that it appeared that his hands had touched something solid and he tugged on it. He pulled and strained till his face grew red. After a moment, she got behind him and helped by pulling on his belt. She couldn't very well just let someone work like that right in front of her. They started to gain some ground and their feet inched backwards slowly. Anomalie's eyes were screwed shut as if to keep the pressure of her exertion bottled up inside when, suddenly, they popped backward onto the floor with Anomalie splayed awkwardly behind him. She quickly hopped to her feet, embarrassed. She looked forward to see what they had been tugging at, and there before them was an exact replica of the container that lay open on the other side of the room, only this one was much smaller. Sigil quickly began to busy himself with the interface to the device. She watched, her curiosity aroused, reasoning that at the very least, he wasn't Judicial so he couldn't be all that bad. After a moment, the cover of the box cracked open. A hissing noise came from it as its lid slowly rose and Anomalie found herself leaning forward in spite of her misgivings. Lying peacefully in the container was a tiny dark-haired girl. Anomalie was thunder-struck. She could imagine a strange man falling prey to the holos and believing in the virtual media that was pumped into them day and night, but she couldn't believe that anyone would bring a child down into the Bunkers. She was about to spin about and lash out at him, even if he did have a rifle, when the girl opened her eyes. Anomalie stopped and stared, the girl's face blossomed into a smile and she felt drawn into smiling in reply. Intuitively, she saw that the smile was not meant for her. Looking over her shoulder, she saw the eyes of the man behind her as he focused on the little girl in the container. He saw that she was conscious and he bent to lay a restraining hand on her to stop her from rising too quickly.

He spoke before the other two could. "It looks as though we have made it, Mara. Anomalie? This is Mara Worth. She is six years old and she is the single most important person on the planet."

THEY SAT in Anomalie's room in the Bunkers; she listened as Sigil talked and she tried to piece it all together. The story that he told was decidedly at odds with the version of history that she had been taught in school.

"I knew it!" she exclaimed, "I knew there were too many gaps in their story. It just didn't make any sense. When I found all of these artifacts here in the Bunkers, they were totally not in the curriculum. I was taught that all of the feeds were Judicial. That the media had always been one hundred percent Judicial. That the war was a police action designed to keep the economy stable. That we owe our lives and livelihood to the Judicial Monarchy." She looked as if she was about to spit. "The very existence of all of these songs and art and stories..." She gestured to the piles of relics strewn around her. "They claim that this never existed. But I know the truth."

Sigil nodded and picked up a magazine from the floor. "This is America, Anomalie, or what's left of it post Culture War," he said. "Over a century ago, there was a war fought in the worst, most inhumane way you could imagine. It culminated and ended quickly; the small units of the resistance were all but overwhelmed. But the war wasn't over land or resources or religious dogma. The war was about culture, indefinable pieces of text, sound and images. Art, music, literature, even dance became increasingly relevant as the information age progressed. As the second and third worlds attempted to squeeze into the first, commodities such as food or water or shelter became devalued. Intellectual properties such as trademarked or copyrighted materials became more valuable than life itself. This was all orchestrated by the founders of the Judicial Branch."

"Branch?" Anomalie interrupted. "You mean Monarchy."

"In the beginning, the Judicials were simply a branch of a typical twenty-first century government," replied Sigil. "But, under the influence of Thomas Worth and his cult, they grew in power, and always focused on the regulation of cultural data. For a time, creative work enjoyed a renaissance, basking in the glory of great economic power. In time, this became decadent, leading to increasing corruption and eventually, protracted hostilities. The violence was unprecedented, triggering a genocidal backlash against the creative artists themselves, a punishment they were not entirely innocent of causing. In the aftermath, any creative output was harshly restricted. Various warlords, under the protection of the corporate cartels and the Judicial Monarchy, controlled vast empires of creative content, building immense networked catalogues and stables of indentured artists, all tightly controlled for the use of Judicial propaganda."

"Vids and propa-spins..." mused Anomalie.

Sigil nodded. "All other artistic endeavor was illegal. It was into this environment that you were born."

Anomalie thought about what he had said and a question rose in her mind. "If you two were down here during the end of the war, then how do you know all that happened after? I don't get it. Really, who are you two?" Mara was playing by herself in the corner of the room. She had headphones on and was going through piles of tapes one by one as she looked at flyers from long ago concerts.

Sigil replied to Anomalie's question with a broad explanation. "Mara and I are throwbacks to an earlier stage of evolution. You are what we would progressively evolve into. Or rather devolve." Anomalie ignored that last remark and Sigil continued. "And for us, time doesn't work exactly the same as it does for you. Mara and I are here for a reason and I have a question of my own." He paused. "How did you ever become so different from the others around you?"

"I was always different. My 'plants never really worked right, you know? It made things harder for me at school. I was never stupid, even though some people thought I was, it was just that we were poor, and my dad used to knock my 'plants around." She put her chin in her hands and leaned forward onto her knees and rolled her eyes up to a poster on the wall. "I tried to hack better gear when I could, as soon as I was old enough, but good silicon is hard to come by and you can't teach yourself very fast with a malfunctioning net chip. A vicious circle, you know? Lots of times, I had to learn things the slow way, by reading. I just couldn't keep up with the direct feed with such a choppy signal, so I kind of drifted off on my own after a while. I started to come here. Here, in the Zone, nobody's implants would work right, nobody can get by unless you can think. This is the only place where I'm not the crippled one. It's illegal, you know." Sigil looked at her, questioning. "To read about this stuff," she said. "Music, and art, and stories. It's against the law. If your 'plants work, they'll block the input of free data. Mine just let this junk right in."

Suddenly, Anomalie's face brightened as she recalled how Sigil had introduced Mara. "Did you say Mara *Worth*? Like Thomas and Solomon Worth?" When Sigil nodded affirmatively, she let out a low whistle. "The heads of the Judicial Monarchy? She's related to them? Those two are really bad news...I mean it. They are not the sort of people that you want to tick off. Each one is worse than the other. How is she related to them?" When Sigil explained briefly, she nodded with a bemused expression. "She's his sister? The old man's daughter? Oh, I get it, time travel, paradox and all that. I keep forgetting that the two of you have been out of the loop for a while. This just keeps getting weirder and weirder."

Sigil gestured at the room and spoke to Mara, "Is Anomalie the girl from the picture in the hallway, the one near the stairwell? Is this Corrina?" Mara shook her head mournfully, for she knew that Sigil would continue to seek the girl from the painting and that he would never recognize her until after she had vanished. She looked deep into Anomalie's eyes. Anomalie felt as if she was under a great telescope, as though the eyes that were inspecting her came from a great distance and from very high above her.

She swallowed nervously and turned on her defense mechanism. "Oookay…enough of the Twilight Zone stuff for one day. I don't know how much of this I can take in at one sitting. Who is Corrina? If you don't start giving me some kind of straight answers, I'll call the Judies on you myself." In spite of her threat, she was actually more intrigued by these two odd strangers than by any other people that she had ever met. Her curiosity was eating away at her patience, and she could sense that Sigil and Mara were there to do something important. She was there with them for the same reason. She was nervous and excited and apprehensive all at once, and she had no intention of returning to her grid, her street, her apartment, her father, or her life until she had some idea of what was going on.

Sigil looked despondent as he heard the news from Mara. He recovered quickly though and turned to face Anomalie. "Corrina is a problem that only I can solve, if, indeed, there is a solution at all. It is my curse alone, not yours or Mara's." He gazed at Anomalie for a long moment, pondering. "I, for one, am very interested in you and just how you fit into this drama. If there is one thing that I have learned as I've traveled through the stream, it is the fact that nothing happens that is not part of the script. The Most High does not allow it." Anomalie looked uncomfortable at the mention of spiritual matters. Sigil saw this subtlety and moved through it. "We will need your help in finding any-one in this place who would be willing to help us. Besides yourself of course." She looked at the two strange compan-ions standing before her and saw them through the eyes of a regular citizen.

"Right... You two are certainly not going to blend in. Let me think." She paused and thought for a moment. "Well, there's always the Crax."

"The Crax?" asked Sigil.

"Yeah, the Crax. The colloquial term for the under-ground. Get it? Fallen through the Crax? The misfits that navigate that zone are unstable, to put it mildly. Af-ter the grids lost contact with the artists and writers, we thought that maybe they were all gone. They weren't. At least not completely. The ones that were left were ummm... unpredictable, I guess. They knew that their only hope for survival was to sever all contact with the Judi-cial Grids entirely. This meant that they became fugitives, hunted down. Crax people are intelligent and resourceful though, and they don't give up that easily." She shook her head, a grim look on her face. "I don't know, though. They can be dangerous."

"So we work on establishing some form of communi-cation with the residents of the Crax," replied Sigil. "I'm sure I knew some of those people from the start of the fight-ing. When the original strikes and raids were executed, the creative types formed small pockets of resistance and kept off the main grid, we were never completely sure how they did it. They were somehow able to keep telnet style comm up and running even though the Judicial Branch had cut off power and had jammed or encrypted all terminal con-nections. I think that they were using some sort of high-frequency data transfer, like through ham radio style setups. My theory is that they had managed to overcome the limitations of the narrow bandwidth and were able to create independent nodes of terminals. These wouldn't have relied on traditional net connects and wouldn't have required the Judicial infrastructure. I'm not sure, but that's what I think. Thomas and Solomon Worth will keep a close watch on anyone that has influence in that community. That might be the first place we could start to look for them."

Anomalie's mouth hung open. "*Look* for them? Why in the world would we *look* for them? Are you completely nuts? I'm not going into the Crax! Not on your life! I've heard stories about Judicial Rangers that have been lost on patrols just near the borders of those areas; you don't even want to hear the rumors. I don't want to wind up like that, taken by some wacked out savage bohemians in the unlinked regions. I'm not going in there, no way." Anomalie was obviously shocked by the suggestion.

"You have no choice," Sigil replied. "Our only chance is to link up with someone from the Crax, that's it. That's all. You...we...have no choice. And we don't know if those rumors are true or if they're 'savage bohemians' at all. We have to at least try."

"I guess you're right...maybe," answered Anomalie reluctantly. "But I'm not reciting poetry...or relating my feelings, or chilling with any dirty hippies. Not on your life."

"Okay, no dirty hippies, I promise," he returned. "You never know, maybe they'll be just like you, obnoxious, precocious, wannabe punk chicks." He watched Anomalie bristle.

"Hey! Watch yourself, mister! You don't know just how obnoxious I can really be yet. Push my buttons and I might just show you."

ANOMALIE STOOD with Sigil and Mara at the border of the Old Zone and watched the sun rise over the concrete ruins. She had retrieved what few possessions that she still valued from her apartment and crept out while her father was still sleeping. She had returned late in the evening.

"Have you settled everything with your friends and family? Have you said good-bye?" Sigil asked. Mara held Anomalie's hand in one of her own, her other hand was twisted tightly into Brownie's fur. She looked up at the older girl and squinted as the first rays hit them together. Anomalie glanced at the unearthly soldier who still remained an inexplicable mystery and quickly looked away.

Her voice was almost too low to be heard. "I don't have any friends or family, at least not any who will care. Not anymore. My friend Colleen is in the hospital, I found out yesterday." Her voice trailed off, then rose again. "They said it looks bad."

Sigil put his hand on her shoulder. "I'm sorry," he said.

"Don't be," she replied. Her jaw tightened as she put her backpack down next to the others, one immense and one tiny. "It was only a matter of time, I could never get her to listen to me..." Her eyes were wet as she set about arranging her pack. "I don't ever want to come back here. I'm never coming back here." Her voice choked slightly at the end and Sigil chose to politely ignore it. He stayed silent. Mara held out Brownie for her to hold. She took the bear and sat down in the dust next to the little girl. She looked up at the gray hooded man and asked, "Why is this happening to us, why is it hard like this?"

Sigil looked out at the expanse of destroyed urbanity and pondered her question. "All of humanity has asked those questions for ages. You know that, don't you?" he said.

She replied quickly. "The two of you came from a place or a time where there were answers, you were there when it started. Let me in on it."

He thought for a moment and nodded. He sat on his pack and spoke in a soft voice. "I was there long before it started, Lee-lee. Mara was there with me. Long before the wars of your people were scarring and burning your Earth, we saw the seeds of conflict planted." He seemed as if he was speaking to himself more than in response to her request and so she stayed silent. She was afraid that if she were to interrupt, he might not finish his thought. She shifted on her pack as if it were delicate china, as if any disturbance would burst the bubble of his memories. "I cannot show you, or explain," he continued. "Just trust that the path set before us is walked for the good of all, and that there are forces arrayed to stop us that are even more powerful than any that you have encountered. We must stay close…and keep faith."

The three sat on their packs, Anomalie's arms wrapped around the small, strange dark-haired girl as she thought about the trials that lay ahead of them. Even Mara, in her innocence, remembered the night that she had met her father and felt his imposing presence. She felt the absence of her brother for the first time in her life. All three knew that their path was set and so they focused their hearts on the struggles of the coming days.

Chapter 20

Epilogue

THE MORNING LIGHT was beginning to seep beneath the tavern door as the old storyteller wound down his tale. Those who were gathered around him turned their heads and saw with surprise that the new day was dawning. They collectively blinked their eyes and stretched their arms and backs. Reluctantly, they settled back into the world that they knew so well. The innkeeper was the first to shatter the spell.

"That is quite a tale, old man…" he began. "I'll venture that we've heard none like that." The old man sat back on his stool and looked down at the floor. None of the company knew what to make of such a fantastic story. They looked at the traveler in a new way, seeing a deeper strength in him; he was honed to a keener edge. He seemed larger and more solid than he had the night before. The fire had burned away and no one had noticed; it had been some time since it had been fed and outside the tavern, the morning birds could be heard, starting their early songs. The gathered audience seemed to draw a collective breath and, together, they began to form a question. Before they could speak though, the old man raised his head.

"I see that the night wasn't big enough to hold such a tale…" he said. "They seldom are. Perhaps the dangerous road that led me to your fine establishment and to the company of you fine folks is less treacherous in the glare of sunlight." He stood and moved to the door. The people sat still and silent as they watched him reach out and pull the door open, letting the cold morning sunlight into the tavern. They winced as the harsh brightness struck their eyes. The old man stood at the threshold for a moment and considered the path that had led him there. Once again, it was the innkeeper who took the plunge and cracked the silence.

"Wait…" he said. "There must be more. What happened to the children? To the gray man? How is it that you know these things? You said that this story was yours." His voice betrayed his eagerness and the eyes of the people showed the same. The old man hesitated and turned to face the gathering. He looked them over carefully.

"Yes, there is more to the tale. Much more. I wonder, do you feel that I paid a fair price for a bed and a meal?" There were unanimous nods and gestures all around, the old man stepped back into the inn and closed the door behind him.

"I am old," he said, "and cannot do many of the things that I could in the past. Spinning tales can sometimes exact a heavier toll than miles of wayfaring or days of combat. Before I can pay the remainder of my bill, I must rest." The innkeeper nodded and motioned to his wife. She moved from her position behind the bar and started to lead the way to the stairs. The old traveler followed. Wide-awake, the innkeeper's children scampered behind him like curious kittens. At the foot of the stairs, the old man turned and faced the room. "It will take some nights to finish the tale, it spans over many years. It is not only my tale, it is each of yours as well. I thank you all for such hospitality and for your gracious ears. At nightfall I will begin the tale anew." And with that, he went to his room and closed the door.

-End Of Book One-

Author's Notes

*Or, how I went about writing such a thing
and where it goes from here.*

When I was completing this revised edition of Onlyness, I toyed with the idea of completely rewriting this note to you, the reader. In the end, I decided to republish the original Author's Notes in its unchanged form, warts and all. Although the book has been edited enough to warrant a new edition, the meat of the story remains largely intact and my vision for the characters remains clear. The revisions were generally focused on continuity and tightening the timeline of the Judicial Rising, in preparation for the events in the next book, The Right Hand Path.

So, here they are, exactly as printed in 2008.

THE ORIGINAL concept for these stories came from a musical score that I was writing. In the traditional operatic or ballet libretti, a composer would utilize an already established story. Tchaikovsky used The Nutcracker and Swan Lake, Berlioz used Romeo and Juliet. Many of the famous fairy tales had been redone within the ballet or the opera. I decided that it would be better for me to write a new fairy tale, something that was more contemporary and reflected the sort of music that I would put to paper. The initial notes sat in various notebooks, stored in boxes throughout my apartment for years. Eventually, I found myself in something of a financial bind. I had just recorded a set of about twenty-five pieces of music, both classical and contemporary, and I couldn't afford to finish mixing or mastering them. I looked frantically around my studio for an idea and my eyes came upon these notebooks. They were filled with lyrics and poetry that would usually have ended up in songs. Many of them were too whimsical or emotional to be used in the type of music that I would normally be performing, which was punk rock or hardcore, so I thought, "Maybe I can sell some of this stuff." None of it was anything close to a novel and I was certainly not a novelist; I simply thought that some of it might be worth something to someone, maybe as a short-story submission or an entry in some kind of poetry contest. I had nothing else to offer so I decided to go for it. I looked around for publishers that might be interested but I didn't find any that interested me. As I let the material percolate, the poetry started to connect to the softer lyrics and all of it began to form a tentative plot.

I've alway been a pretty serious comic fan and I first looked at the plot as something that could be serialized, a set of characters that would develop over a period of years. Anomalie was certainly a character that I thought of as becoming a great comic heroine. Her unique abilities could be a twist on traditional super-heroines and her political motivations could develop into something more mature and thought provoking. I thought that the relationship between the siblings Solomon and Mara could become something strange and eerie and that they would grow into adults continously discovering more about their powers and history. Sigil was a character that needed to be redeemed for some deep wickedness in his past that occurred on a greater than human scale. It was at this point that I realized that maybe I could write a *book*. This is quite an arrogant position to take, I believe.

In order to justify taking the time out of your life to write a novel (or two, or three), you have to weigh the time spent writing against the potential income lost. Are you going to be able to make financial sense of the whole endeavor? If you're unpublished and you say yes to that question, you're basically saying that you believe, for some arbitrary reason, that people are interested in paying money to read what you write. I think that's pretty arrogant. But then again, people buy an awful lot of books. I really didn't have much of a choice, I had to sell something to someone or I wouldn't be able to continue to write music. So, I went for it.

Now, thinking about writing a book, and actually writing a book are widely different experiences and I smashed my way through this first one with vigor. I learned a tremendous amount in the last year and I now think that I could finally write a real novel. The problem is that I wrote *this* one! I have much more in store for our heroes. They face the real guts of the story in the coming books and I hope that they gain enough friends along the way to justify the time spent because it, sadly, is time that can't be retrieved. I, of course, will be spending *my* time with them and seeing this adventure through to the end. I hope that some of you will see it through with us.

J.A. Wynn

www.ingramcontent.com/pod-product-compliance
Lightning Source LLC
Chambersburg PA
CBHW070009120726
47909CB00003B/850